The
Magical Christmas

Do Over

By

Linda West

Morningmayan Publishing
Morningmayan.com

Dedicated to my mom and dad,
James and Constance West
RIP Dad
I still miss you everyday.

It's the Christmas season, the happiest time of the year! Before we begin, let's get you settled in with a cup of cocoa and a comfy chair.

Let's imagine a crackling fire is beside you casting a warmth and glow. Perhaps a light snow has begun to fall outside. When Christmas is upon us and joy fills the air, we remember that all good things are possible.

So sit back, relax, and have a nice drink. You're about to take a wonderful fun-filled adventure with the adorable inhabitants of the Christmas-obsessed town of Kissing Bridge. Now on to the story.

I hope you enjoy it. Sending you love and cheer and mistletoe wishes. May your days be filled with Christmas cookies and kisses...

With love,

Linda West

Just released Christmas 2019!

"Once in a blue moon you get a chance to change your life, and this was that blue moon."

CHAPTER 1

It was a cold December eve, some say the coldest in decades, and a blizzard warning was in effect. Being the Friday before Christmas, most of the workers at Kennedy and Crane had already left for the Christmas holiday.

Samantha looked at the clock and groaned inwardly. It was after eight o'clock, and she wanted to go home like everyone else, but her boss, Macy Kennedy was in an extra foul mood even for her.

"Shouldn't you be getting home to put on that awesome Chanel dress you bought for the big night Macy?" Samantha chirped brightly trying to lighten her up.

Macy spun around and glared at her with daggers in her eyes.

"No, I shouldn't be getting home to try on my Chanel dress." She mocked Samantha's syrupy tone.

Her dark brows were knit together and her brown eyes looked black with the size of her pupils. She ran her hands through her short, dark hair and then stared back at Samantha with disbelief.

"I got a text from Todd an hour ago. He's gone off to LA with some friends *for Christmas!*"

Samantha's mouth opened.

"What? Why? Didn't he –" She stopped herself. "I'm sure he has a good reason, Macy."

Macy snorted.

"Yeah, good reasons usually don't come in a text. I'm losing him, Sam."

Macy plopped down in her chair and stared out the large picture window at the oncoming storm. She tapped her long, manicured nails on her desk like a woodpecker. "Says he'll call me when he gets back...in a month."

Samantha's mouth fell open. Poor Macy. It looked like she was getting the ultimate big let down, broken up with at Christmas. No engagement celebration after all.

"Here's a piece of mail you didn't get." Sam said quickly, as she placed it on Macy's sleek metal desk. Mail usually distracted Macy.

"Send it back." Macy said dully without turning.

Samantha continued hopefully. "It's not the annual Christmas invite from your mother Macy, that one is always in a red envelope. I *always* send that back. This is something different."

Samantha looked at the pretty Tiffany blue colored envelope. "It's addressed to you personally, not the company."

Macy cocked her head to one side intrigued.

Sam rushed on eager to bring some sort of happiness to her boss. "Maybe it's a love letter from Todd with two tickets to Paris for when he gets back?"

Macy let out a big huff and gazed out the window at the sheets of snow beginning to fall.

They both knew that wasn't the case. Todd's last minute text was just a breakup in disguise.

But if not Todd, then who? Macy really didn't have any close friends that would send her a Christmas card. Anyone that did know her knew she abhorred Christmas. Too much money being spent in the name of sentimentality and tricky marketers as her father always said.

Macy waved her hand without looking back at Samantha as if she were a servant.

"Read it."

Samantha scanned the letter, then suddenly, caught her breath and brought her hand to her heart.

"Macy."

Something in Samantha's tone made Macy spin her chair around.

"What?"

"It's from a friend of your mothers, a Ms. Carol Landers."

"What? You have got to be kidding me?" Macy threw her hands up in the air. "Now my mother is having her friends write me to beg me to come visit her? How utterly selfish!"

She shook her head. "What is it with her? She ruins my life and then she stalks me. Can't she see no matter how many times she begs me to come home for Christmas, *I'm not going to Kissing Bridge!*"

Samantha swallowed uncomfortably and croaked out, "I'm so sorry, Macy. But this letter says that your mother passed away yesterday, and you're the only relative left to claim her body."

She looked up sadly and met Macy's stunned eyes.

"You have to go home to Kissing Bridge."

Chapter 2

Macy felt an odd sense of nothingness. Instead of sorrow there was a vague grayness that didn't nearly match the depth of feeling called for. Maybe it was regret. Her mother, dead. She hadn't even known she was sick. Then again, she hadn't seen or spoken to her since she was a child. Her mother's big, kind brown eyes flashed across her memory, and she swallowed hard.

She picked up the letter Samantha had put down in front of her and read it.

"Dear Macy, I'm so sorry to tell you that your mother has passed away. Nobody

seems to have any contact number for you, and I pray that this letter finds its way to you by the grace of God. Please come home to Kissing Bridge to collect her remains because we don't know what to do with her body.
Sincerely and with great sorrow,
Carol Landers."

Macy didn't move for a moment, and it seemed as if time stopped.

Even in death her mother was managing to ruin her life. She closed her eyes to shut out the truth, and squash down all of her feelings, like a fly that needed to be swatted.

Feelings were weakness her father had always taught her. Feelings hindered your life, not helped. Stick to the bottom line, work hard and it would pay off. That was his motto. When it had become hers she didn't know. She felt a panic attack coming on again.

Just then, the maid opened the door and walked into Macy's office, not realizing people were still in the building. Happy holiday music followed in her wake through the crack in the door and her jaunty red bell earrings jingled as she walked.

"Oh!" She stopped dead at seeing the big boss and her personal assistant still at the office. "Sorry! I thought y'all were gone like everyone else in the building."

Macy spun her chair around, her brown eyes flashing in anger. She glowered at the poor woman and looked her up and down, trying to find the source of the tinkling, festive sound.

Macy pinched her dark brows together and rose from her chair, pointing at the offenders hanging from the maid's ears.

"There!"

She turned her anger on Samantha. "Don't we have a company employee dress code?"

Samantha looked the maid's outfit over. She was in the company mandated black uniform with her name, NAOMI, scrawled under the Kennedy and Crane logo.

Samantha straightened. "Of course, Macy. She's wearing black that's the holiday dress code. I sent out memos to the entire staff. I don't see the problem."

Macy pointed at Naomi. "Those – those holiday earrings look ridiculous. It's an embarrassment to the company."

Samantha's eyes widened. "I'll make sure I add it to the original memo and send it off after Christmas, Macy."

The maid looked at Samantha with fear in her large, almond-brown eyes, and she fidgeted, not sure what to do next.

Samantha waved her in further. "It's fine, Naomi. Please come in. Do what you need to do. We don't want to stop you from getting your work done just because we're working overtime."

Macy started pacing across the room like a panther. She was dressed in all black and thin as a rail and looked like she was ready to explode.

She turned her attention to Naomi, who was busy dusting and trying to finish up as quickly as possible so she could make her way safely out of the office and Macy's weird Christmas ire.

"Naomi."

Macy read the nametag and addressed the maid as if seeing her for the first time.

Naomi King stopped and lifted her beautiful eyes to look Macy in the face. She had been working for the office-cleaning agency for five years now, and she'd run into the strict and serious Macy before, but never had been regarded, let alone talked to, by her.

"What are you doing for Christmas? Kids, gifts, all that I guess?" Macy prodded. "Figgy pudding maybe?"

Naomi cocked her head to the side. She didn't need the big boss lady asking questions or giving her the super-stare down right now.

"Got one kid. He's in jail, so I guess I'll go by for a visit. Bring him some cigarettes."

Macy stopped pacing and looked at her.

She was sorry she asked.

A new weather alert suddenly erupted from Samantha's Apple watch and startled her. She pushed at the side controls trying to shut off the irritating warning buzzer reminding them the blizzard was almost upon them.

"So Macy, shall I try and book a flight for you?" Samantha asked. She was bewildered by Macy's lack of reaction to the death of her mother.

"Kissing Bridge, Vermont right?"

Macy nodded. "If I have no other choice."

Naomi spoke up. "There's no way you're getting an airplane out of here. It's been all over the news that all the flights have been canceled for the next three days due to this darn blizzard-of-a-century coming in."

Samantha parried. "Okay, a rental car then."

Macy shook her head. "Like no one else had thought of that alternative on the Friday before Christmas."

Samantha countered. "Right, of course. A car then. I'd lend you mine if I had one, Macy, but who has a car in Manhattan?"

Naomi piped in. "I do."

They both looked at her.

"How much?" Macy said dully.

Naomi cleared her throat. "Well, it's actually my boyfriend's pickup truck, so I'll have to call him."

Samantha shut off her watch and sighed. She had already gotten three warnings on her phone about the oncoming blizzard. She was eager to get home like everyone else, but it rarely mattered what Samantha wanted.

Samantha Henderson just did what others requested.

She had survived her entire life that way, and the last ten years of being the Boss-from-Hades' right hand lady.

Everyone else who had ever had the misfortune of working for Macy Kennedy was fired within months, sometimes weeks. One poor girl never made it through the first day. But if nothing else, Samantha was a survivor.

The law office had moved uptown, Macy had been made partner, and Samantha followed and kept her head down. Partially to avoid the caustic moods of her temperamental boss, but also to shield her facial deformity from curious eyes.

Samantha was a natural beauty, with large green eyes tinged with dark lashes and cheekbones to die for. Her hair was a soft blonde and it hung nearly to her waist, with long side bangs styled perfectly to mask the left side of her face as much as possible.

Still, if one looked a bit closer, they would see that the side of Samantha's pretty face was smashed inward all along the left side of her face, with a maroon lighting thin scar that ran the length of it.

It didn't make Samantha ugly, but it made her strange.

Unnatural.

Different.

It wasn't people's faults they stared. Sam had come to understand that people did that when they encountered something they weren't accustomed to. She had gotten used to the staring over the years, but the damage to her face was not the worst of her disabilities.

Chapter 3

Naomi rang her boyfriend and clenched her hands. It'd been a few hours since her last session, and she hadn't expected the bosses to still be hanging around the office at this late hour. She usually had the place to herself, and she could pop her pills while no one was looking.

Once she was high, Naomi felt normal and able to go about her mundane, thoughtless routine of cleaning the affluent offices of Kennedy and Crane until the wee hours of the morning. After that she would go home to her big dose and the awaiting peace of slumber before it started again.

Where was that loser Kiki? Totally like him to *not* be around when they had a sweet deal like this just fall into their laps. If she worked this right she could get a ripe good deal out of Ms. High-and-Mighty Kennedy.

Kiki picked up.

His voice was hoarse and he sounded out of it.

"Kiki," Naomi whispered urgently despite the fact that she was alone. She looked over her shoulder. "I got us an epic setup to make some easy cash off my psycho boss woman. Her momma done croaked and she needs a ride home."

Kiki seemed to brighten. "And? What's it got to do with me?"

Naomi released her breath. "I need your truck for a couple days, until Monday at the most."

"No way."

Naomi knew only cash and his next pill purchase, which often went together, motivated her boyfriend.

"She'll pay five hundred bucks," Naomi lied.

She planned to ask Macy for a lot more than that, but she wasn't about to let that on to Kiki. She knew Macy was over the barrel with no options and she planned to milk the situation for all it was worth.

Naomi had a kid in jail that the lawyer said he could help if she only had the money. She was going to ask Macy for two thousand dollars, help her son, and maybe get a little place for herself that didn't include Kiki.

CHAPTER 4

Naomi returned to the office. "He said he'd be happy to help."

Samantha brightened, but Macy glowered at her. Clearly the thought of six hours of driving to pick up her disowned mother's body was going to be too much for her to handle.

... "but he wants two thousand," Naomi finished.

Macy let out a big laugh. "Of course he does. Not like I have any options! Right, Naomi?"

Naomi cast her big almond eyes down.

"Not really, ma'am."

"Have you heard of price gouging?"

Naomi looked at Samantha, then back at Macy. She shook her head. "No, ma'am."

Macy threw her hands up. "Well, it appears I have no choice, so go get this golden vehicle I'm renting us for the exorbitant price of $2,000 and let's go!"

Samantha looked up. "Excuse me? Us?"

Macy waved her off with one hand. "Go home and pack. Naomi, you too. Then come get us in this rented chariot and let's get on with this miserable nonsense."

Samantha caught her breath. "But – but it's Christmas weekend, Macy! We spend it with Harold's parents every year. I can't –"

Macy patted her on the back. "Afford to lose your job? We both know sweet Harold doesn't make enough as a dental salesman for all those tests you need."

Samantha's eyes flashed with anger and she bit her tongue so hard she tasted blood, but she kept her face calm. How dare Macy use that against her? She'd only told Macy the truth of her condition because she'd burst into tears last week over the failed results again, and the impending future of not having enough money to retry in vitro fertilization.

Samantha decided she was *just going to say no*.

"I'm so sorry, Macy, but I just can't go. Christmas is really important to Harold."

Macy glanced up.

"I'll pay you twenty thousand dollars to go with me, Samantha."

She rose from her seat, walked over, and took both of Samantha's hands.

"Handle this for me…. Please Sammy. I can't do this without you. And you need the money; you know you do. Maybe this time it will take?" Macy's eyes softened as she stared into Samantha's green orbs. "I know how much it means to you both. Harold will understand."

Samantha shook her head. This was so typical. Over the years, Samantha had put up with untold difficulties being Macy's right hand girl. Harold thought she was horrible, and begged Sam to quit years ago. But Samantha had outlasted eight of Macy's boyfriends, three best friends, and twenty assistants. By default, Samantha was possibly the longest relationship Macy had ever had.

Sam took a deep breath. She knew Macy meant well, and that she hid her vulnerability underneath all her bark and bite. Even though she came across as harsh and cold, Macy had a good side down deep, very deep, inside.

Samantha softened. Poor Macy had just lost her mother.

"I'll have to talk to Harold."

Macy nodded. Naomi opened her mouth to complain, but Macy put a hand up to stop her.

"And before you go saying no and leaving us alone with your boyfriend's jalopy – I'll pay you an additional $3,000 to drive us up there and back."

Naomi's eyes went large. "You got yourself a driver."

CHAPTER 5

Macy closed the bathroom door behind the girls and lit a cigarette. She wanted to cry. Everything in her wanted to cry. But Macy Kennedy had stopped crying a long time ago. Her body shook and she raised one trembling, finely manicured hand to her mouth and took another long drag.

She talked herself down off the ledge, as she felt another panic attack beginning to rise. She was supposed to take long deep breaths if she felt a panic attack coming on, according to her therapist. But Macy found a cigarette always worked too. Gosh darn her mother.

Images of her mother flashed in her mind. She had so few memories from the short time when her parents were still together.

Her father had married her even though she was simple, and perhaps mentally unstable. But he didn't want Macy's life jeopardized by the division of worlds. He had moved Macy back to Manhattan with him and cut off all contact between them.

It wasn't until Macy had moved out on her own that the letters started coming.

For every special occasion, her mother had sent a card, even on Halloween, for Pete's sake. It seemed any minor holiday, even Labor Day, was a reason to contact her estranged daughter.

Maybe she was as crazy as her father claimed.

Lately, Macy feared she herself might not be all that healthy of mind, body, and spirit either. Her weight had plummeted to a scary hundred pounds, and makeup barely covered the dark shadows beneath her eyes.

Her relationship with Todd had been floundering for months, and despite her urgency to control and focus their romance into a firm commitment, it had been the basis for a number of fights.

Macy had thought they were on track for a relationship merger, as she liked to call it, and they had finally agreed and chosen a large diamond engagement ring at Tiffany's for Macy, which she had agreed to pay half for.

She took another deep inhalation of her cigarette.

They had picked tomorrow night because it was Christmas Eve, and a full blue moon. A rare occurrence and a perfect backdrop to the beginning of a perfect union. Or so she had thought.

She wanted to cry. She wanted to feel. The years of being taught to be an emotional soldier by her headstrong father had taken its toll and she was just like him. Rich, successful, and unhappy.

She stubbed out the cigarette.

Time to pack and get ready to go to the town she had successfully avoided for the last twenty years, because she could avoid it no more.

CHAPTER 6

Samantha fought to keep the jalopy truck with improper snow tires on the road up the steep mountains to Kissing Bridge, Vermont.

It was snowing so badly, Samantha could barely see in front of her.

She struggled to see through the snow storm with the old truck lumbering up the the hill slowly.

Kissing Bridge Mountain was high up in the clouds and possibly had the worst weather of the entire state of Vermont. It was also stunningly beautiful.

Macy was terrified from her position in the back seat. She had her fingers clenched against the door and was screaming every other minute. "Watch out! Be careful!"

Sam rolled her eyes and gripped the wheel tighter.

Naomi had passed out asleep and was currently snoring as she leaned against the window with her coat bunched up for a pillow. Luckily for her she had slept through most of the whole scary ordeal up the mountain.

Samantha finally pulled the truck into the parking lot of the Amigone Funeral Home. Despite the heavy snowfall and freezing temperatures, the parking lot was completely full.

Chapter 7

Macy looked around the room at all the faces she didn't know, and finally at the one she did. Her mother's body was laid out in a simple casket. People lined up to leave flowers and kneel and pray. Macy hung at the edge of the crowd, far away from the body of her mother, afraid to go closer.

The funeral parlor was hot with everyone crammed in, and an elegant black sign simply said LENORA KENNEDY by the entrance door. As they slowly inched closer to the casket, Macy stopped. Samantha squeezed Macy's hand; she could see her boss was on the verge of a breakdown.

They proceeded closer, and Macy's face turned white. She looked at Sam for strength, then down at the still body of the slight woman in the casket.

"She's so small," Macy said absently.

She didn't recognize her. Her eyes had been what Macy remembered most, kind and warm. They had been the same color as Macy's, but now they were closed forever.

"I need a cigarette," Macy said, and she bolted off toward the exit with Samantha in her wake.

Naomi was already in the lounge area by the backdoor. She was on the phone, talking in hushed tones, and she walked out into the cold and away from Macy and Samantha when she saw them.

Macy fumbled with her cigarettes.

"I can't wait to get out of here. Seriously, I need a drink. Samantha, locate the nearest bar and let's go."

A unique looking elderly woman with a flaming red beehive that rose two feet in the air came over to the small group.

Samantha noticed the woman's eyes were red from crying. A white cotton hanky was clutched in her hand.

Her intense blue eyes penetrated into Macy's coal brown-black ones. Macy took a deep inhalation followed by a long, slow exhale of smoke and studied the strange lady with bad hair.

"You must be Macy," she said. "I'm Carol Landers, your mom's dear friend..."

Macy took another drag of her cigarette.

Samantha held out her hand and shook Carol's in a professional manner.

"You're the woman who wrote the letter?"

Carol nodded. "Yes. I am so grateful you received it. Thank you so much for coming; it means so much... I mean, it would have meant so much to Lenora."

She dabbed at her eyes with the hanky.

Macy turned her back on Carol and stubbed out her cigarette.

Samantha cleared her throat. "It was so kind of you to put this all together. You mentioned there were accommodations available – Macy's mom's house?"

Carol bobbed her red beehive up and down. "Yes, yes, of course. It's all taken care of – but you weren't planning on leaving so quickly? I'm sure your mother's friends would like to meet you! We've all heard so much about you, Macy, but never met you..."

Macy eyed the old lady with the flaming red beehive. She was smiling sweetly, but there was definitely an undeniable accusatory undertone in her voice.

Macy focused on adjusting her scarf and avoided Carol's probing eyes. Gosh darn this do-gooder. How were they supposed to escape neatly with this nosey friend of her mother's stalking her? Macy didn't care for her attitude or her undeniably blaming undertone. She obviously didn't know what Macy had had to endure growing up with a mother that was so crazy she couldn't cope with caring for her only daughter. This lady with the shaming look in her eye didn't know what it was like for a little girl of five to be plucked from what she knew and left with the Kennedy family and all that that entailed.

Carol must have decided that Macy was not worth her time and dismissed her. She addressed Samantha instead.

"There's still the matter of what to do with her body."

Macy turned around, irritated with the passive-aggressive small talk.

"Look, can you just handle this? You were her friend, right? I don't really care to make these choices. I barely knew her when she was alive."

Carol's sympathetic blue eyes hardened and she drew herself up to her full height, a good six-foot-five with her massive beehive. She suddenly reminded Samantha of the goddess Athena ready to do battle.

The senior glared at Macy with open hostility and Samantha stepped back at the look in her eye. Sam didn't know who scared her more, Macy or this sweet old lady looking like she would rather see Macy in the coffin than her friend.

"Well, I'm so sorry your mother's death has been such an inconvenience for you, Macy," she said with a coldness that matched the temperature outside.

"We all appreciate you coming home – even if it had to be under such sad circumstances. I loved your mother, but the choice of what to do with her remains is a family matter."

Macy glared at her, but Carol was no shrinking violet. She glared right back with equal intensity.

"Look," Macy said in exasperation. "I can see that you don't think very well of me. And you're right that I never did come to Kissing Bridge to see her, but this is not my world! Look around at these people."

Macy pointed to a woman in a pale green, shapeless dress and cheery red cardigan with Santa embroidered on it.

"I mean seriously, I wouldn't be caught dead in that outfit even cleaning my floor – not that I would clean my own floor!"

"Well," Carol continued, "it's your loss." And with that, she patted Macy on the back and turned away.

Macy looked at Samantha, puzzlement clouding her face.

"Did she just shun me?"

Samantha's eyes went big. Carol Landers had indeed just given her boss the unofficial hand.

Macy was indignant. "How dare she!"

Macy walked after the retreating older woman. "Hey!" Why she felt the need to make this ornery friend of her mother's understand her side of things was a mystery.

"Carol! Hey, old lady, I'm talking to you."

Carol Landers Archibald stopped and turned. She looked at Macy with open disdain.

Macy defended herself. "I'm not a horrible person. Really. I wish I would have come back to see my mom before she died. You don't know the whole story. Don't you think I would have given anything to have gotten to know my own mother?"

Carol let her speak. Her blue eyes stared into Macy's dark ones, and Macy could see she didn't believe her.

Macy said, "I mean it! Don't you think if I had the chance I would do something different? That if I could do it all over again, maybe I would choose something different?"

Carol challenged her. "Would you?"

Macy tossed her head in agitation. "Is this a trick question?"

Carol raised her eyebrow. "Let's just say it's an option."

Macy let out a harsh laugh and snapped her fingers. "Boom. I magically get to go back and get a do-over?"

Carol nodded. "Something like that."

"Okay, I'll play your game. For one, if I had my wish, I certainly wouldn't be standing here in Kissing Bridge where I've successfully avoided going to for twenty years."

Macy looked at Carol defiantly.

Carol walked closer to Macy and peered deeply into her eyes. "I'm so sorry that your mother's death has been such an inconvenience for you, Macy…" The repeating of those cold words hung in the air and dripped icicles. "But if you truly meant what you said, if there is somewhere inside of you, a place in you that really wishes that things could have turned out differently between you and your mother…well, I'm willing to help you with that. I loved your mother and it broke her heart not to see you."

Macy swallowed hard. How this old lady with the crazy beehive was making her feel badly about herself was bewildering.

Carol scribbled an address on a piece of paper. "Here's the address to your mother's house, and here's the address to our bakery. Go get a cookie. Tell them Carol sent you."

CHAPTER 8

"Thanks for the great help, cookie lady," Macy said rudely.

Carol smiled. "Oh, no problem, darling. Make sure you get one for each of your friends as well."

Suddenly she changed back to a sweet old lady and was no longer the Mr. Hyde she had appeared to be.

"Just be prepared when you eat that cookie to make sure that you think a lot about the exact Christmas you want to do-over, because you only get one second chance."

Naomi had come up to the group just then. She looked around in confusion at the situation and raised an eyebrow. "Are we going to eat?"

Macy finally lost it. She started laughing manically. "What are you talking about, old lady?" She looked back and forth between the girls. "Is it just me, girls? Or does this sound nuts?"

Samantha lowered her tone. "Macy, don't be disrespectful."

Carol's mouth turned up in weak attempt at a smile. "Oh, I know dear; it's a lot to wrap your mind around. Things are different in podunk Kissing Bridge. But it is a blue moon Christmas, and it might be the chance of a lifetime. "

With that, Carol glanced over and winked at Samantha, then walked away.

The girls plodded back to Naomi's boyfriend's beat-up old truck, bent on getting away as quickly as possible. But the snow had fallen and gathered hard over the last hour. The vehicle was now covered in a shroud of white flakes, and the snow came up clear to the fender.

Samantha looked at Naomi. "Do you have a shovel?"

Naomi shook her head. "Why would I have a shovel?"

Samantha took in the situation. "We're not getting this truck out of here."

Macy hissed under her breath. "Call a cab, Samantha. I'm hungry. Let's go find a place to eat and a decent drink. I'll be in the truck smoking; let me know when it gets here."

Samantha made the call, but it was useless. She shivered and snapped her cell phone shut. The mountain reception had been barely audible, but she had gotten the message loud and clear.

She knocked on the truck and Macy opened the door and let out a big mouthful of smoke that froze as it left her mouth.

"The cab company said it would be over an hour before they could send someone."

Macy opened her mouth to complain and Sam put up her hand. "But good news – there's food just down the street that is supposed to be wonderful. It's a short walk."

Macy pouted in response.

"There's wine," Sam taunted.

Macy wouldn't budge. The pout got bigger.

"Freeze or food: your choice. I'm picking food." Samantha started walking and Naomi ran after her. Sam looked at her. "You're quick."

Naomi smirked. "Quicker than you know, girl."

Macy finally dragged herself out of the truck and followed them, mumbling to herself about how lame Kissing Bridge was.

The three girls made their way from the funeral home parking lot down to the small main street sidewalk that had luckily been recently shoveled. They neared the gaily-lit shops of midtown. The snow was falling again heavily, but the old-fashioned, cast-iron streetlights, swathed in wreaths with bright red bulbs, cast a subtle glow. The light spilled out over the bright snow, creating a gay warmth.

As they approached the main center of town, rooftop speakers rang out happy holiday tunes. The gaiety was in direct contrast to the bad weather. Gusts of wind sent sheets of snow flying towards them as they shielded their eyes and continued to push forward.

Samantha pointed up at the *Landers' Bakery and Enchanted Café* sign swaying in the winds.

"Food!" she announced triumphantly.

They ducked into the bakery. It looked warm and inviting, and the girls hustled in as much for food as for cover. The door swung shut with a bang and a whistle of wind.

The *Landers' Bakery* was a lovely cabin-styled shop with heavenly aromas and a cheery fireplace aglow in the corner. The place was full of people chatting amiably around long wooden tables as if at a big party. The TV on the wall broadcasted the news, and the reporter was announcing road closures and other casualties of the "blizzard of the century."

The buzz died down. Suddenly everyone stopped their bantering and looked up at the newcomers like they were bizarre birds that had landed amongst them. Someone snapped off the TV, and a strange silence enveloped the room.

The girls looked at each other uncomfortably.

From her position behind the counter, a feisty-tempered, fair-haired lady with snappy blue eyes waved for the crowd to move. The customers waiting in line at the cashier parted like the Red Sea.

The attractive senior looked the girls up and down, slowly and silently, while the crowd observed. She finally called out to them.

"I take it you're the girls from New York City."

Naomi gazed at the crowd now all staring at them and waiting for a response. "How the heck could you tell that? We just darn walked in the place?"

The blue-eyed woman looked down her nose at the crew that had landed in her abode.

"*All black* clothing at Christmastime? You're *not from Kissing Bridge*."

The bakery crowd nodded and murmured.

The whole room was full of locals, and they donned Christmas-appropriate garments: red, green, reindeer, and Santa appliques thrown in with some holly and ornaments. One girl was dressed up in a complete elf outfit with a hat and jingling bell.

Macy opened her mouth to let them all know that black was *always chic* when the lady added,

"And my sister, Carol, told me you were coming."

Macy snapped her mouth shut. Not another of these incorrigible Landers women!

She let out a loud sigh. This sister probably knew her mother as well, and thought Macy was a horrible person too.

Samantha cleared her throat. "We've driven quite far and could use a full meal if that's –"

Ethel Landers came out from behind the bakery display case and smiled sweetly at Samantha.

"Let me show you over to the Enchanted Café side, dear – right here through the doors. They're still serving dinner."

She looked back over her shoulder at the other girl behind the counter with the big violet eyes and a curious expression on her face.

Ethel eyed her intently. "Kat," she addressed her helper, "would you grab some of our special cookies for the ladies to take later for dessert?"

Kat looked at her boss Ethel and they both touched their noses and started laughing.

Chapter 9

The girls were stuffed from an amazing meal, and two empty bottles of wine stood on the table. Most of the other guests of the Enchanted Café had braved the storm and headed home. The staff was cleaning up, and it looked like the restaurant was prepared to close.

Ethel Landers came over to the table. Samantha couldn't help but note how attractive she was. Suddenly, as if reading her mind, Ethel turned to her.

"I think you are a very pretty woman."

Samantha blushed, and swept her hair over the damaged part of her face instinctively.

Ethel smiled at the group. "I hope you enjoyed your dinner, but it looks like we need to close soon. They're expecting an extra bad cold front with the blizzard almost upon us."

Naomi looked out the window and her eyes widened. "We're not going to get snowed in like one of those adventure movies where everyone gets all cannibal-like, are we? What was that film?"

Samantha cut in. "That was the Donner Pass, and no – we'll be fine, but we should probably get back to the house and get settled in."

Macy threw her black credit card onto the table. Ethel looked down at it.

"Thank you," said Ethel. "And these are for you."

She put a pretty Tiffany-blue bag down on the table.

Macy looked at the bag.

"What's in that?"

Ethel eyed her. "Cookies."

Macy laughed. "Boy, you guys are really pushing the cookies here in Kissing Bridge."

Ethel continued. "Well, they have been blue ribbon winners for over fifty years –

but's that's not the point. My sister, Carol, said that you needed the Magical Christmas Do Over cookies for very special reasons."

Macy unfurled a slow, slightly drunken smile. These yokels were nutsy and cute, kind of. She could see how her father could have been originally charmed by their sweet naiveté. Macy might as well indulge her.

"Yes, we've come all the way from Manhattan for the special magical cookies."

"I'm sure you have, dear." Ethel said sincerely, "More than you know."

Samantha looked in the bag and pulled out a cookie. It was in the shape of a Christmas tree, frosted in white, and had scrolled, shiny silver writing on it that said:

Magical Christmas Do Over.

Samantha blinked in delight.

"These are beautiful! Thank you so much! I kind of thought your sister was joking about the do over thing."

Macy spit out laughing. "Oh, this is rich. I can't believe this!" She was nearly doubled over with mirth. "Oh my gosh, is this really what's been going on in small towns? Samantha, you're not really believing this?"

Samantha looked uncomfortable and then down at the cookies. In a small voice she said, "I think they look beautiful and magical."

Ethel looked Samantha in the eye. "Just be sure to read the directions."

Chapter 10

They could barely see through the oncoming snowstorm as the taxi wound its way slowly through the small town to the turnoff on Mistletoe Lane.

Samantha looked around the cab. "Where is that bag of cookies the Landers sisters gave you?"

Macy looked petrified at the horrible weather as she wiped off the window, trying to see through the blinding whiteout.

"'I left those stupid cookies. Those ladies are crazy. I think it's horrible to foster some false placebo hope that will only leave you sadder at the other end. Thanks but no thanks."

Samantha moaned. "I wanted mine."

The taxi braked at a crooked, snowy trail that led through a sea of pine trees. Macy stuck her head forward. "Why are you stopping here? I don't see a house."

The snow was hammering down hard as the taxi driver looked up at the sky. He hopped out of the vehicle and held open the back door for the girls to exit.

"Sorry, ladies. You're going to have to walk it from here. I'll be happy to help you with the luggage."

Macy rolled her eyes and got out of the car. As soon as she touched the ground, her Chanel black high heels sunk into the white snow bank and she was stuck like glue.

"UGHHHHHH!" Macy tried to free her feet.

The taxi driver looked back at her. "Not much good for getting through the snow in those fancy shoes. You want me to carry you too?"

Macy was slung on the taxi driver's back. He gripped her luggage in each hand. Samantha and Naomi trudged through the snow ahead of them with their own luggage. Macy howled complaints about how uncomfortable her ride was.

Naomi looked over at the young, handsome stud carrying her grumpy boss, and then she looked at Sam and smiled.

"That's what I call a real man. Not to mention his tolerance level."

Samantha nodded. "I think those ear muffs he has on are helping."

After a few hundred feet, the pine forest cleared and the snow lightened. Samantha could see a small house alight in the distance.

Jade green pines surrounded the cabin and were lit with Christmas lights that glittered like tiny stars amongst the heavy snow-laden boughs. The huge blue moon suddenly slid out from behind the storm clouds, illuminating the whole yard and home in all its Christmassy, gaudy glory.

Naomi laughed and pointed.

"Well, look at that. We're staying in Mrs. Claus's cabin!"

Samantha thought Macy was going to faint. Before them was the most adorable, gingerbread-cutout-cookie of a house with Christmas decorations hanging from every nook and cranny, as if it were made to mock Macy personally.

As if this Rockwell picturesque holiday scene wasn't enough to annoy her Christmas-hating boss, the whole festive ordeal was topped off with a gigantic two story, bright red blow-up Santa in the yard.

Naomi shook her head. "I'm getting the idea that Macy and her mother were nothing alike."

Samantha brought her hand up to her mouth to stifle a laugh.

Macy roared in agony.

"You've got to be kidding me! There is no way I'm staying here. Samantha, read that address again!"

Before Sam could assure her they were at the right address, suddenly Carol Landers burst forth from behind the huge blow-up Santa with a hearty wave and a welcoming smile on her face.

Macy moaned loudly at the sight of her.

Carol greeted them happily.

"Oh, dears. I'm so sorry. I realized I had forgotten to give you the key to the house before you left."

Chapter 11

Carol opened the door to the house and flipped on the light. The interior was simple and homey and filled from top to bottom with Christmas decorations, including a large tree that nearly groaned from the weight of its many ornaments.

Macy was disgusted. She looked about, horrified by the absurd amount of decorations that had been shoved into this shack of a house. "I can't believe she lived like this in this hovel! I can't stay here. Samantha, find the best hotel in the area."

Samantha was about to tell her she had already checked for hotel arrangements (everything was booked up) when Carol chuckled.

"Don't bother. We only have one place to stay here on the mountain, the Eagles Peak Lodge, and it's been booked for ages."

Macy moaned as she looked around again. "This is all she had? Who could live like this? My father was right; she must have been crazy."

Carol looked at her. "She was happy, and she led a simple life. I don't think she thought she was wanting for anything."

Samantha went over and looked at the tree. "How beautiful." She examined some of the ornaments. "These are handmade?"

Carol nodded. "Yes. Lenora was a wonderful artist. Teacher too. She taught an art class right out of the front sunroom here. The kids will really miss her. Can't say we have a replacement...and poor Conner is overwhelmed."

Carol opened the door to the studio and Samantha followed. Samantha was enamored with the sunroom and its art. It burst with all sorts of easels and childlike paintings midway done, and she could just imagine how beautiful it would look with the midday sun beaming in through the big picture windows.

Naomi went off to find the bathroom, with a bottle of pills in her hand.

Macy was in the front room, tallying up the problems she had to deal with. "Sam, we're going to just have to donate all of this junk. None of this stuff is even sellable unless someone's into white trash style." She touched the old couch and a bit of dust puffed up. Macy made a prune face and wiped her hand off on her black slacks. She still had a grimace pasted on as she filed into the front sunroom.

Macy looked at the children's paintings and brushes scattered about and hung up on the walls. Samantha pointed excitedly to Macy. "Oooh, these are fabulous, Macy. I can see these in your office."

Macy looked at the large, brightly colored abstract paintings with interest. They were good. Better than good. They were brilliant. Macy considered herself a connoisseur of art and was a frequent visitor to gallery openings about town.

Macy looked over at Carol, who seemed to be watching her too closely for Macy's comfort. "These are very good. Did my mother do them?"

Carol shook her head. "A student, actually."

Macy's face fell. She had so hoped to find brilliance in her mother *somewhere* instead of the shame she felt for her mother's sad, pathetic life. "Oh well. I saw the K signature at the bottom and just assumed. In any case these might work in my office like you said Samantha. I guess you never know where you'll find greatness..." She trailed off at Carol's expression.

"Well, I best be going," said Carol. "They're expecting three feet of snow tonight; I took the liberty of filling the fridge with some essentials for you."

Samantha smiled and followed Carol to the door. "Thank you, and let me walk you out."

"Oh, nonsense, dear, I'll be fine. Been trudging through snow for nearly eighty years. My husband, Dr. Archibald, is probably out front right now waiting on me."

Carol tugged on her coat and hat and bid farewell to the girls. "Oh, goodness," she said. "I almost forgot." She pulled something out from her bag. "The key to the house and some cans of food for Toulouse."

Macy looked over. "Who's Toulouse?"

Just then, a fat yellow tabby came sauntering out from underneath the couch and wrapped himself around her legs.

Macy screamed.

Carol smiled. "There you are, Toulouse. He's your mom's cat."

She looked at Macy, recoiling as if the cat were plutonium. "Yours now. Be careful not to feed him more than a can a day. Your mom had him on a diet."

Macy looked down at the affectionate fat cat winding lovingly around her legs, leaving little white and yellow cat hairs all over her stylish and expensive black trousers.

"I don't like cats!" Macy declared.

Carol shrugged.

She looked to Naomi and Sam. "Have a wonderful night, ladies." With that, she waved goodbye and then stopped in her tracks.

"Oh! I almost forgot this too! My sister said you accidentally left behind the cookies, so I brought them with me."

Once again, the bag full of magical Christmas do over cookies appeared.

Carol placed them on the table.

This time, Samantha snatched them up for safekeeping.

"Thank you so much! And Merry Christmas!"

Samantha waved from the door and watched Carol Landers trudge down the snowy walk with her red beehive glowing like Rudolph's nose.

Chapter 12

Macy sat on the couch with Toulouse in her lap. She kept trying to nudge the fat kitty off, but Toulouse just snuggled deeper and purred, undeterred.

Macy released her breath and finally gave up. "My father was right! Everybody in this town is crazy! My mother was crazy, that Carol lady with the beehive is crazy, and her sister with her mystical mystery cookies is crazy, crazy, crazy! This is a crazy town!"

Naomi shrugged. "I kind a like it."

Samantha suppressed a giggle and said, "You have to agree that the food at that Enchanted Café was amazing, right? Who the heck makes hard times mock apple pie anymore?"

Macy raised her eyebrows. "Nobody."

Samantha smiled. "I just love your hometown, Macy. It's so friendly and sweet and the people are so nice."

Macy's eyes darkened. "It's not my hometown. I didn't grow up here; my dad got custody of me when I was five, so I grew up in New York."

Naomi saluted Macy. "Anything you say, general."

Macy gave her a scaling look. "Stop calling me general."

Samantha suppressed a smirk, then rose and made some tea. She didn't want to let on to the others just how fascinated she was with the magical cookies. Sure, they were probably fake, but who knew for sure? Maybe they had some special energy that would somehow help her get pregnant or change something.

She loved Harold so much. They had both wanted big families, and it had been devastating to find out she might never conceive. She looked out the window; the snow had stopped for the moment and now the huge moon glowed brightly.

Sam beamed. "Look, it's the blue moon! The second full moon of the month. A blue moon Christmas is supposed to be super, extra, big good luck!"

She pulled the curtains back to let the moon shine in with all its glory. "So what about those cookies?" Sam said.

Naomi shrugged.

"Everything else I ate from those Landers sisters was amazing. I can't wait to eat that cookie; I don't care if it's magical or not. But if it is then I want a full life do over."

Samantha chided her. "Oh, Naomi. I'm sure that's not true."

Naomi chortled. "Are you looking at my life? I'm a maid! I've got a man that won't marry me and a kid in jail. Just how bright does my future look to you? I would do over the whole darn thing! Where are those cookies? I'm eating mine and going to bed."

Macy looked around the irritatingly sweet Christmas-filled cottage and winced.

"This wine isn't doing it for me. I'll be up all night with this horrible Feng Shui. Samantha, be a doll and make me a real drink."

Samantha moved to heed the general's order. She knew her favorite drink when she was upset was a double barrel whiskey on the rocks.

CHAPTER 13

Macy held up the pretty silver cookie and examined it. "I guess I'm drunk enough to try it. What's the worst thing that spiteful old lady could do to it besides maybe throw something psychedelic in there? She wouldn't have the nerve to poison us. Hopefully."

Samantha was studying the note that came with the cookies. "Well, it says to eat it on a full blue moon only, and we have that! Wow, okay, weirdly specific… So we have magical cookies and it's about to be Christmas: maybe a miracle could happen?"

Macy laughed. "I could pass out drunk without taking my sleeping meds if you call that a miracle."

Naomi chuckled at Macy's giddy drunken lightheartedness. "Let's just eat the darn things and be done with it."

"Wait; let's just make sure we follow all the directions." Sam said, ever the perfectionist. "Okay, it says we should be prepared if we choose to change things – that other things may change in our real life when we return." She scanned the note and looked up in wonderment. "They really put a lot of thought into this!"

Macy rolled her eyes.

"Secondly," Samantha continued, "we must concentrate and decide on exactly the Christmas year we want to do over because we only get seven days. The magical cookie will take us back to exactly a week before that Christmas."

Macy got up to pour herself another whiskey on the rocks. Sam raised her eyebrows. Macy must be really drunk to be doing *anything* for herself when Samantha was there.

"How about you, Macy – which Christmas would you do over?" Sam questioned.

Macy smiled back with a tipsy joie de vivre. "Can I pick all of them?"

Sam smiled at her. Macy almost looked happy.

"Sorry, boss, just one. Surely you have one really rotten Christmas that sticks out. I mean, you hate Christmas, so this should be easy for you."

Macy raised her glass in touché.

She mulled it over as she shook the ice in her whiskey.

"I guess it would be the Christmas I thought I was getting engaged –*the first time* – and instead my pro surfer boyfriend ran off with a yoga instructor."

Naomi frowned. "What's the do over? You want to stop him from going off with the yoga instructor? You think he's your soulmate or something?"

Macy waved her off. "No, he was a loser! And I don't believe in soulmates. But he was my FIRST loser. I think I started a bad pattern with him. I was avoiding taking the bar exam, and Thor–"

Samantha laughed. "Thor? Really?"

Macy shook her head. "Yes. Should have been my first warning. In any case, he was everything my father hated. Free spirited, fun, and deep in this ocean cosmic kind of way. He was always telling me I had to find my 'spirit voice.'" She laughed at the memory. "I could just have heard my father. *Spirit voice* – how do you make money off of that?"

Samantha's eyes went wide. "Oh my goodness. Midas Kennedy would have lost it!" Samantha threw her hand over her mouth as her private nickname for Macy's father slipped out.

Macy looked at her oddly, and then started laughing. "That's him, Sam! He would have killed me if he knew about Thor! He hates poor people!"

Naomi made a face and shook her head.

"Anyway, I really wished I would have gone home to talk to my mom – you know, like all the other normal girls that got their hearts broken for the first time." Macy swallowed the golden liquid and its heat warmed her. She softened her face and looked at the girls.

"And if I had gone home, I might have really gotten to know my mom before she got sick." With that, she raised her glass and plopped down on the old sofa.

Naomi picked up the magical cookie directions and gazed at it.

"Well, I for sure know which Christmas I messed my life up."

Both girls looked at her.

"I had this awesome coach in college – he was like a dad to me."

She looked at the two women in front of her, and decided they'd never understand.

"Let's just say I wish I would have asked him for help when I needed it."

Samantha looked at her. "What kind of coach was he?"

Naomi smiled. "Track. I was a top runner. Hurdler too."

Samantha took in Naomi's taut physique. She could definitely see the earlier athlete in her.

"Wow, how impressive! I never knew that about you."

Naomi nodded proudly.

"Well," Sam said as she folded the directions back up. "Shall we all eat the cookies together?"

Naomi stopped her.

"Wait – what's your do over Samantha? You gotta tell us too."

Samantha took a deep breath. There was no question the Christmas she would do over. She hesitated to even recall the events of that time.

Sam looked at the ground, overcome with emotion. She swallowed hard. Sam usually kept her head down, for so many reasons. She didn't like to show her mutilated face, and she didn't like to betray what she felt. Her feelings had been used against her too many times in her earlier life.

But these were broken people just like she, and they had dared to expose the truth of their hearts to her. If she had any hope that these magical blue moon mystical cookies would change things, she had to be authentic.

Samantha lifted her head high and told them the truth. "The night this happened." She pointed to her scar and the bashed indented side of her beautiful face. "It was just before Christmas. I had a plan to get out of a bad situation, but it was the wrong plan, and I got caught... and this happened."

Samantha sucked back the horror of it, and her eyes glistened wet.

Naomi and Macy were silent. Her heart broke at the concern that shone in their eyes.

"I really don't care about my face." Sam said. "I mean Harold isn't bothered by it and he's the only person I care about. But...it's just the accident hurt my insides worse. And well, if I could really get a real do over...maybe I could have children?"

She wiped at her eyes with her sleeve. "Oh, silly me, blabbing on. Let's eat the darn things."

She took a big bite of her cookie.

Chapter 14

Macy sat in the living room of her mother's house and stared at the ugly Christmas decorations strung everywhere she looked. That confounded huge tabby cat that needed a diet was still planted in her lap. If she had been a little more sober she would have gotten up and turned off the Christmas lights that seemed to mock her with their gaiety. Then again, the snowmen lamps were worse.

Macy frowned as she reached over and

picked up the instructions for the cookies. *Magical Christmas Do Over.* What kind of schmuck thinks anybody would buy this kind of crazy nonsense?

The cat suddenly leapt off her lap and walked over to a saucer on the floor and looked up at her expectantly.

Macy looked at him. "What?"

Toulouse looked back at her and meowed. Macy guessed that meant he was hungry. She called out to Samantha to feed the cat, but the lights were out in both of the girls' room.

Macy groaned as she got up from the couch and grabbed the can of cat food Carol Landers had left on the table. She emptied the food into the cat's bowl that had been lovingly painted with his name, Toulouse.

She looked around for the garbage to deposit the tin, and pulled open a number of drawers. She pulled open one drawer, and she froze.

Inside was a group of letters, many with bright red envelopes.

Macy reached in and withdrew the large bundle of letters that were wrapped in a piece of twine as it for safekeeping. She let out her breath. More work to deal with. Clearing out her dead mother's things was something she had no desire to deal with. She'd just let Samantha deal with it.

Macy's name suddenly shot out at her as she went to replace the bundle.

As she looked through the top group, she realized that they were all the letters that her mother had sent her over the many years.

Many of them were unopened, and all of them were labeled – RETURN TO SENDER.

Macy gathered the stack, and sat back down on the dingy divan and looked at the letters as if they were the boogieman. A flash of guilt wracked her.

All of the letters on the top of the bundle had been sent to Macy directly at the company address on Park Avenue, and had all been dutifully sent back by Samantha on Macy's orders.

But her mother had kept them anyway. Why?

Macy randomly pulled a letter from the middle of the bunch and opened it up. This wasn't any recent card…this was older and addressed to their family penthouse on 5th Ave.

She opened it up and looked at it.

It was a hand made Easter card from 1988, and it had a bright pink bunny and happy flowers that had been sewn on by hand with patches of quilted fabric. On the inside it simply said,

"Happy Easter Darling Macy,
I wish I could be with you. I hope you're happy.
I love you, your Mom."

Macy tore open another one; it was a Christmas card from 1993 with a jolly Santa on it.

"Merry Christmas Darling,
I wish we could be together and I hope you love the presents Santa brings you. Come home anytime we can make cookies together.

Love, Mom."

Macy quickly rifled through the plethora of letters and cards that were still unopened.

There had to be over two hundred of them. ALL ADDRESSED TO HER.

Macy took another long drink and stared at the star on top of the overly decorated Christmas tree. How come she had never been told about these letters?

Of course she knew about the Christmas invites begging her to come home that had started arriving at her business, but Macy had already hardened her heart against her mother by that time.

She hadn't trusted her mother's pleas to see her. For most of her childhood she had been told her mother didn't want her. That the responsibility of having a child was something she just couldn't handle. Macy assumed she must want something from her to be so persistent after the fact.

Yet, if she couldn't believe her emotions, she could believe evidence. Macy stared at the stack. These letters were real proof her mother hadn't forgotten about her, and that she had tried to contact her.

She reached out for another letter and opened it. 1985. Macy pulled out the handwritten letter and read...

"Dear Macy,
Happy Birthday, my darling. Seven years old! You are such a big girl now. I miss you so much! I hope to God that you're getting these letters and that you think of me sometime. I know you must be living a wonderful life to be too busy to see me or write back to me, but please know I love you and I'm always here if you ever want to see me.

Love,
Your Mom."

Macy dropped the letter and stared numbly out the window. The snow had stopped for the moment and the huge blue full moon cast a bright light that now illuminated the yard outside as if it were daytime. The newly fallen snow shone pure and white against the huge red blow-up Santa Clause in the front yard.

Macy's head was swirling and she clutched at her heart. It was all so surreal. All these years she had blamed her mother, hated her even. But, it was all built on lies. Her father had had his way, and Macy and her mother were the collateral damage. Finally Macy knew the real truth, but now it was too late.

For the first time she could remember, Macy cried. The tears flowed down her face and she let them fall in abandon.

Toulouse looked up at her concerned and let out a consolatory meow in understanding. He nuzzled his nose into her arm and looked up at her with his big hazel eyes. Macy petted his soft fur and her eyes roamed over to the table and her half eaten magical cookie.

Macy's hatred for Christmas had in part, stemmed from her mothers love of it. And now she realized she didn't have anything to fight. All of her anger had been unwarranted and misplaced.

She finished the cookie and washed it down with the rest of her whiskey. It had been one heck of a tough day and she was a little drunker than she'd planned, but perhaps it was better that way.

She gathered up her mother's fat cat and a blanket and snuggled down on the couch and looked at the Christmas tree. It was oddly comforting now and a perfect symbol of her mother. Toulouse purred and cuddled in deeper next to Macy, and soon she was fast asleep.

Chapter 15

Christmas 1995
A week before Christmas

Macy awoke in an unfamiliar room. She looked around. A simple bedroom. White eyelet coverlet and a poinsettia on the side table. Where was she?

She glanced out the window and recognized the mountains of Kissing Bridge.

She rubbed her eyes and got out of bed. Odd. She didn't remember even getting off the couch last night.

She pulled the curtains back and looked out the window; a lovely new blanket of snow covered the ground and the glorious mountains surrounding the town sparkled like aquamarine gems.

The smell of bacon cooking reached her nostrils and her stomach rumbled in response. She usually only had coffee for breakfast.

Macy wrapped a robe around herself and made her way down the hall to meet the girls. Somehow, having company was a comforting thought and she felt excited to see her comrades.

Then a weird feeling hit. Something was different. Sure, they had come in late and she had only seen the house lit by the hideous snowmen lamps on the end tables, but things looked really different.

Now the place seemed less rundown and sad. Instead, it felt homey, sweet, and warm. In the corner was an old iron fireplace, and it crackled and spit as flames licked the logs.

She stood in the dining room and looked around her mother's house. The kitchen looked brighter and happier than it did yesterday. All the gaudy, overdone holiday decorations were gone too!

Where were they?

Macy rubbed her head. How many drinks had she had last night?

Macy heard someone humming and climbing up the stairs from the cellar.

Suddenly, *her mother appeared in the kitchen*. She had a bowl of fruit in her hand, and she put it on the kitchen counter and got busy paring some apples as if she hadn't a care in the world.

Macy gasped. *Her mother.... in the kitchen?!* She must be dreaming!

She looked just as Macy remembered as a child: a sweet face, petite stature. Her light hair was fastened in a high ponytail, and she had an old fashioned apron tied about her waist.

Macy looked down at herself. The skin on her arms; she hadn't been this tight and muscled since her 20s! She ran to the hall mirror and looked at her reflection.

Oh my goodness, she looked 25 again! Macy's big brown eyes went wide in amazement. This was the most vivid dream she had ever had!

A brief flash of those crazy friends of her mothers with their magical cookies and bizarre beehive hairdo rushed through her head.

There was no way those kooky Landers sisters could *actually have* magical capabilities…could they?

Macy's second thought was that it was probably some kind of hallucinogenic. Maybe that nasty Carol had slipped in some kind of wood mushroom into the frosting that had magical properties and she was dreaming this all up right now. Her mother turned to her and smiled warmly. "Good morning, darling!"

Macy inhaled deeply and tried to remain calm.

She rubbed her eyes, bent on waking herself out of this dream. Her mother began rolling out pastry dough. "Are you hungry?"

Macy struggled to find her voice in this bizarre fantasy. Her mother looked at her and sensed her vulnerability. She dusted her hands off on her apron and walked over to Macy. She enveloped her daughter in a strong, warm embrace. They hugged for a long time, and neither of them let go.

"I know it's hard to make small talk, darling. It's been so very long. I just want you to know I love you so much and I'm so very happy you came home to Kissing Bridge for Christmas."

Once again, Macy felt her eyes fill with tears. She reached up self-consciously and swept them away. She must be losing it.

But it didn't *feel* fake. It felt real.

"I missed you, Mom," Macy said sincerely. Her mother hugged her tightly again and they both cried for the time they had lost together.

Finally, her mother pulled back and wiped her own tears away. "Goodness, I've prayed for this for twenty years, and when I get my wish, all I do is blubber! What you must think of me."

Macy looked at her mother's kind face. "I think you're wonderful. I – I found the letters…"

Her mother seemed confused. "Letters?"

She didn't seem to understand.

She thought it best to let the discovery of the undelivered letters be shared until a later time. Her mother was looking at her intently.

"How are you feeling today, sweetheart?"

Macy felt a pang of deep regret.

Thor.

Todd.

Constant abandonment.

Thor's parting words rang in her head as if it were yesterday. *You're cold, Macy. You love money more than you could ever love me.*

She would hear echoes of that same phrase from every succeeding guy that ever walked away.

Macy looked up at her mom's concerned face and dared ask the question that gnawed at her. "Mom…am I just…. unlovable? I think something is wrong with me." Tears trembled on the edge of her eyes and Macy wiped them away angrily.

Tears are weak, her father always said. Kennedys don't cry.

Lenora Kennedy put her hand on her daughter's heart. "I know it hurts, darling – it's good to let the tears free. Your tears are like rivers that break through the dams we erect to keep ourselves safe but they never do. Let the tears go, my love; your river of feeling will bring you back to the ocean and connection of life."

Macy had no idea what kind of Yoda like wisdom her mother was spouting right now, but she was looking at her daughter with true love in her eyes.

Oh my gosh, Macy thought, *this woman loves me for me!*

"Mom, why didn't you fight for me when I was younger? I was so alone. I needed you – I blamed you..."

Her mother's face softened. "Oh darling, I wish I was stronger."

Macy's eyes flashed with anger. "I know my dad is intolerable, but why didn't you just come get me?"

Lenora rose silently and went to an old roll-top mahogany desk. She opened it and removed a package.

Macy looked at it questioningly; it was the group of letters she had discovered in the drawer...was it only yesterday?

Her mother looked at her sadly. "Last week, I received these from your grandmother. I had no idea you had never got them...I thought you loved your life and that...you were better off without me."

She shook her head. "I never thought you weren't receiving them. I should have known better."

Her mother swallowed. "Your father put a restraining order against me to stop me from contacting him. But I only contacted him because I couldn't get through to you! I just wanted to see you, talk to you, and make sure you were happy. I tried to fight him and get custody of you; I got the best lawyers I could afford..." She shook her head and regret filled her beautiful eyes.

"My money ran out before the Kennedys' did."

Macy's eyebrows rose in surprise and understanding.

Her father's family had used their power and money to control her mother, and ultimately her. Of course they did. That was their mode of operation.

All these years she had thought her mother just didn't care enough to bother, and she had been forcefully and legally kept away!

For the next two hours, Macy and her mother made up for the time they had missed together.

They shared the special moments they had missed in each other's lives, and Macy relived her whole youth to her mom over cookies and three boxes of Kleenex tissues.

She poured out the whole sordid tale of her repugnant love life gone bad and how unhappy she was in her life in general. She hated the thought of being a lawyer.

"Well, if you don't want to be a lawyer, darling, don't be a lawyer. You're old enough to choose your own path now."

Macy shook her head. "Mom, you are so much braver than me! Dad would never forgive me. Besides, how would I live? What would I do for money? I'm spoiled. I have a penthouse with an expensive mortgage and I have a brand new Mercedes; do you know how much a brand new Mercedes costs?"

Her mom shrugged. "I usually take the bus or one of my friends picks me up."

Macy studied this petite lady who was living in a completely different world than hers. Other than the matching brown eyes, they were so different.

"Do you have any aspirin?" breathed Macy. "I'm getting one of my...my headaches."

Her mom scurried up and fetched some aspirin. She handed her the pills and a glass of water.

"Why do you get headaches, honey?"

Macy downed the pills. "I've had panic attacks since I was a child. I don't know if it's stress; the doctor says stress, anyway."

"Well, maybe I can help you with that while you're here, darling. I know some wonderful alternative therapies instead of pills. Doctors never really cure anything, they just put Band-Aids on."

Macy smiled at her mother's optimism. Thousands of dollars' worth of therapy, tapping, acupressure, reiki, and an astrologist had not been able to get rid of the stress that seemed to be Macy's middle name.

"I'll just take some breaths, walk a bit." Macy inhaled deeply. "And maybe have a quick smoke outside."

"Macy!" Her mother exclaimed in disappointment.

"I know, I know, I'm going to quit. But right now I really need one. It helps with my nerves."

Macy grabbed her Chanel blazer (that they insisted was a jacket but barely kept a breeze out) off the coat hook. She put it on over her bathrobe and ducked out the front door. It was freezing outside, and Macy fumbled with the lighter with her cold, clumsy fingers.

She gazed around the snow-laden yard while she pulled in the soothing smoke.

Something was odd. The huge blow-up Santa that took up half the yard yesterday was missing too.

She stubbed out her cigarette and came back into the warm house. Her mom was in the kitchen making more coffee. Macy called out to her.

"Mom...what happened to all your Christmas decorations?"

Her mother looked at her oddly. "What decorations?"

Macy gulped remembering that was *yesterday*, another time – had things changed all ready?

She caught herself.

"Well, it's Christmas in a week and you don't have any decorations up yet. You love decorating for Christmas!"

Her mother seemed puzzled.

Macy hurried on. "I mean, when I was a kid, we had tons of decorations. I remember making the little manger set – we painted it – the ceramic one."

Her mother's warm brown eyes lit up. "You remember that! I wasn't sure what..."

She stammered a moment then admitted, "I stopped celebrating Christmas after you were gone. It was too hard."

Macy's eyes met hers. The depth of their mutual loss registered completely, and bonded Macy even closer to her. She had had so much pain around her mother issues, as Dr. Bombay had said. And for what? Her mother had been suffering just the same.

Macy walked into the kitchen and reached out and grabbed her mother's hands. "Let's get them out now."

Soon, Mom was back with a box full of items, and a couple cups of hot chocolate. Macy pulled out an ornament. It was a tiny handprint – hers – and it was tied with a red ribbon.

She smiled. "You kept this?"

Mom smiled too. "Your first art piece? How could I not?"

They laughed. Macy felt happy and at peace as she watched her mom rise to add another log to the fire.

"How about some Christmas music, Mom? It's awfully quiet in here. Do you have a stereo?" Mom nodded and pointed to the radio in the corner.

Soon "Here Comes Santa Claus" was playing, and they were both spread eagle on the floor across from each other like little kids going through the box of old holiday memories.

There were cards, stockings with their names on it, and a few random tree ornaments.

Macy hummed. "Mom, there's not nearly enough ornaments to decorate the Christmas tree."

Her mother turned from the oven where she was removing some fresh baked cinnamon rolls.

"What tree?" she asked.

"Exactly!" Macy chastised.

The doorbell rang and Macy looked at it with trepidation; perhaps some ghost of her future would be there and whisk her out of this amazing dream.

She opened the door carefully, and a group of small children came rushing in, bundled up in winter gear and all talking at once.

One redheaded freckled girl missing two front teeth smiled and said, "Where's Mrs. Kennedy?"

Macy's eyebrows rose as she saw a tall, dark haired man ushering more children out of a van and toward their front door.

"Mom, there's a bunch of little short people at the door they're asking for you?"

Lenora came to the door and laughed. "Oh goodness, I had forgotten all about art class today. The kids usually come after school, but we're on the holiday vacation schedule."

Macy watched with curiosity as her mother herded the children inside and toward the sunroom where painting easels were set up. The children chattered away as they hung up their coats and put their boots in the milk crate.

Macy's eyes widened as she got a closer look at the handsome man that was rounding up the rest of the small crew and shepherding them toward the door. He had a strong jaw and eyes the color of warm grey flannel. Macy blushed as he caught her full body appraisal and smiled.

He stuck his hand out. "I'm Conner Anderson. Nice to meet you."

Macy suddenly realized she was in her pajamas and robe. She pulled the thin robe tighter around her and stuck out one hand awkwardly.

"Macy Kennedy."

Conner's dark brows rose in understanding. "Well – looky here. I've heard your name so many times and now I get to make your acquaintance in person. Nice to meet you, Macy."

Macy really felt stupid. He had obviously heard of her. He probably thought she was a horrible daughter, never coming to visit her mother all these years.

Her mother came over as she fiddled with her art smock and tied it on.

"Conner – I see you've met my Macy."

Macy smiled weakly as Conner looked her up and down.

"I sure have. And she's as pretty as you said she was."

Macy's mother beamed. "Why don't you come in and stay a while and I'll get you some fresh coffee?"

Conner looked at his watch. "Well, I could use some of your coffee, Ms. Kennedy. Don't mind if I do."

The children obviously knew what was going on because they got to work right away, taking down easels from the storage and setting up canvases and paint and cans of water. Macy looked around. "Mom, you're teaching a painting class?"

Just then, Macy was almost bowled over by a running back in the form of a small boy. "Sorry, Miss Kennedy's Daughter. I need the bathroom."

He spun around and ran toward the door. Macy laughed in spite of herself.

Her mom was chatting amiably with the gorgeous hunk as she poured him a fresh cup of coffee in the kitchen. Her mother waved her over. "Oh, Macy, come chat a minute with Conner. He's the school guidance counselor slash angel of Kissing Bridge."

Conner laughed at her description.

"Don't be painting too fond a picture of me, Mrs. K. Someone might want me to live up to it." His eyes danced and two deep dimples hugged his sexy mouth.

Her mother turned to her and lowered her voice.

"I forgot to mention, Macy, that I have a gathering of children that come here that don't have a place to go. Some are having a difficult time. I teach them art."

Macy clutched her robe around her nightgown. "That's great, Mom," she murmured, fully aware of the hunk of man filling up their small kitchen. "I'll be right back."

Linda West

Macy ran upstairs and rummaged through her things, looking for something appropriate to wear. Everything she owned was black.

She certainly was the odd one out in this sparkly, funky Christmas-obsessed wonderland. She finally settled on a black t-shirt and black jeans. She ran her hands through her raven bob and it fell into perfect place as if trained.

She looked at herself in the mirror and sighed. Gosh, youth looked good on her. She didn't really need any makeup, but she applied some mascara and lipstick anyway, then stopped herself.

Who was she getting dressed up for? For Pete's sake, she didn't need to go get herself all worked up over the first nice looking guy she met. That's all she would need is to fall in love with a small town nobody and live out her life in an oblivion like Kissing Bridge Mountain.

Still, Macy sprayed some of her expensive perfume on her wrists and neck before she went back downstairs.

Chapter 16

Samantha closed her eyes and lay on the old quilt bed at Macy's mother's house. Through the window, she could see the peaks of the surrounding mountains highlighted by the enormous moon now blazing high in the night sky.

She wished beyond anything that she could go back and turn things around. She had never told anyone the whole truth of what had happened that horrible Christmas Eve in 1995.

She had tried to escape the sorry excuse she had for a life, and had planned to run away with the love of her life and leave all her sad memories and reality behind in Detroit.

But the getaway had gone wrong, and her life had changed forever because of it.

She was seventeen, young and in love with the most handsome boy at school, Riley Demure. Back then, her love for Riley, and their mutual love of acting, had been a lighthouse of hope.

Something deep inside her, perhaps sheer survival instinct, had pushed her to rise up and choose a healthy life, and when Riley had suggested they run away together to California, she had said yes.

They had made a plan. She had packed, and had wrestled between her love of freedom and her duty to her younger brother and sister. She'd be leaving them in the same purgatory she was running from.

But Samantha had reasoned that if she became a Hollywood star, well, she could buy them all a big house and come back and swoop them both up. They could all live happily ever after in the sun and warmth and safety of California.

Riley had revved the engine of his car and pulled away, and Sam had leaned back in the passenger seat and sighed.

That's when she had seen the flash of pink in the rear view mirror.

"Stop the car!" Sam had screamed.

It was her two-year-old little sister, Trulie. She was barefoot and crying, dragging her little pink baby blanket behind her like a life preserver.

Sam had no idea how Trulie had found her, or how she had managed to walk herself so far from home without a coat or shoes.

She had jumped out before the car had even come to a full stop, and scooped up the little girl, bundling her in her pink blanket and wrapping her coat around the child for added warmth.

The little toddler was weeping and sputtering. "Sam...Sam."

Samantha's heart broke.

She had insisted Riley take them back to the house so she could get Trulie safely inside.

But when they had pulled up, Samantha's father had already been waiting for them. He was drunk, as usual, and looked angrier than she had ever seen.

Samantha squirmed as she recalled the horrible events that followed as if in slow motion.

As she mounted the front porch steps with her eyes cast down, her father moved to strike her.

Through a haze of darkness and pain, Trulie had fallen from her arms onto the porch, and Samantha had tumbled backward from her father's hard hit; down, down, down the icy stairs.

All she remembered was the horrifying, tormented scream that sprang from the well inside her, just before she hit the unforgiving frozen ground and everything went black.

Chapter 17

Christmas 1995
A week before Christmas

Suddenly the light hit her.
Samantha blinked at the blinding glare. She seemed to be awake in a dream.

She looked up at the spotlight above her, and then down at herself. She was dressed in an old medieval gown! A bedlam of actors ran back and forth, sets changing, props set up....

Samantha spun around, taking in all the people and moving parts of this mayhem she'd been cast into. She gasped as she recognized her surroundings. This wasn't a dream – or was it?

She was in the backstage of her high school...the play... the night of the final show...the roses in her hands – a congratulatory gift from Riley?

They were in their senior year, and Samantha was playing the lead across from her real life boyfriend, Riley Demure.

Sam caught sight of herself in a mirror and brought her hand to her mouth in awe. She was stunning and normal!

She stared at her reflection; she looked so young and beautiful in her Juliet costume.

Samantha slowly ran her hand down the side of her face that she had gotten so used to hiding. Now it was flawless. Not broken, not scarred or deformed.

Just perfectly normal.

Was she really back in time? If this was a dream, she had never experienced anything so vivid before. She could smell the flowers in her hands, and hear the sounds of the audience awaiting the next act.

The back of the stage was aflutter with activity as the curtain was about to rise. Actors running to and fro in different stages of dress. The director – Dan Blocker – pacing back and forth.

She smiled as she looked at him. Dan would go on to be a very popular documentary director. He had always been serious and determined, even in high school. He caught her looking at him and blew her a kiss for luck. "You're going to kill it, Sam. This is your night!" He hurried off and started an argument with the set designers about the way the turret looked.

Samantha spun around in bliss. These had been some of the happiest times in her past life. Suddenly she felt strong arms around her and heard a familiar, sexy whisper.

"Never forget I'm your Romeo and you're my Juliet, forever and forever."

It was Riley "Ready for the big monologue, my Juliet?" His easy laugh brought a smile to Sam's lips.

She turned and faced Riley. He was looking as beautiful as she remembered.

His dark hair glistening, his eyes that misty gray blue, and even more handsome in his Romeo attire.

She batted her big green eyes. "What you talked about – us leaving – you meant that, right?"

Riley squeezed her. "You want to talk about California now, before we even go into the second act?"

He chuckled. "Yes, we're going to California, beautiful."

Samantha smiled. This time, things were going to be different.

The curtain rose, the crowd cheered, and Samantha looked out over the packed audience from her perch on the mock castle balcony.

She breathed a deep breath, filled with the joy and hopefulness of acting again. She had a whole new future ahead of her.

Chapter 18

Naomi swallowed the pills. Somehow they made all the sadness in her life seem not so bad. Magic cookies. Right. She needed a miracle to fix her life.

Naomi snuggled back on the old bed and thought back to that fateful Christmas where things had spiraled off in a way that she would never be able to control again.

She had been training hard, knowing that the Olympic trials were coming up in a month. This would be her chance of a lifetime.

Coach West had warned her not to push herself, but Naomi was headstrong and determined. She was going to make something out of her life. Not only had she been the first person in her city to receive a scholarship, but Naomi truly had a gift from God. She could run like the wind. In fact, many thought faster than that.

At first, her running had started as pure self-defense. The streets at home were dangerous, and loitering meant becoming a victim. Speed was her protection.

Soon running became Naomi's therapy. Pumping her muscles boosted her confidence. She had joined the track team while others kids were robbing 7-Elevens for extra cash and thrills. Naomi just ran.

By the time she was in high school, she was running the hundred-yard dash in almost world-record time. By her first year in college, she officially passed the world record mark, making her the unknown, but possibly fastest, woman in the world.

According to the trial times and her amazing coach, she was a sure bet for the U.S. Olympic team, not to mention the gold medals. Coach West had faith in her, and she had the heart of a winner. Together they were unstoppable.

Naomi's eyes got droopy, and she finally started to drift away into the peaceful slumber the pills always brought. A smile played around her lips at the thought of Coach West and how proud he had been of her the first time she had passed that finish line and her own personal fastest time.

According to Coach West and his time watch, faster than anyone on record.
Together they had mapped out a plan to the Olympics, which included the right

food, training, sleeping, and of course keeping her grades up. The official qualifying trials would be later in January after the holiday vacation.

Despite her coach's warning, Naomi had thought there was nothing wrong with training harder and longer.

Against Coach West's rules, she was training day and night. Naomi wasn't like the silver spoon college kids; she was a survivor, and a born fighter. She may have come from a poverty-ridden hole, but she was going to rise up and be somebody.

And then she had the accident.

She's been training late into the night, she knew she was tired and should stop, but she pushed on harder. But her legs would not cooperate. Her muscles retracted and her foot got tangled in the hurdle bar. She went down hard, twisting her leg and breaking her ankle with a resounding snap.

She had laid on the black tar track crying and unable to move. Finally a student had found her, and called for an ambulance and gotten her to the hospital.

But the damage had been done.

It was a devastating loss. Her ankle was broken and part of her hip was fractured.

To have such a substantial injury before the Olympic trials was possibly the worst thing that could happen to her.

Chapter 19

The hospital doctors had prescribed heavy medication as the pain was off the charts. By the time Naomi was discharged, the major body damage had passed, but she could barely make it through a day without crying and taking more pills.

It had happened early in the season, and now not only could she not train, but her body was ravaged. She continued to take more and more meds. When the doctor cut her off, she argued with him, explaining how her pain was still significant, but it was to no avail.

The doctor had warned her that she could get addicted to the pain meds, so she had to wean off slowly, which sadly meant dealing with more pain.

He had given her a smaller dose and instructed her to wean down over the next week. But Naomi had finished the supposed week worth of pills by the end of the first day.

Knowing her doctor wouldn't prescribe any more, her boyfriend, Leroy, had gone out to the streets to buy some. It had started so simple and so easy. In Compton, you could find anything you wanted for sale on the corner.

Sure they were expensive on the street, but at least they were plentiful, and sometimes even stronger than her original pills. Naomi didn't have much money, just the small stipend that had gone along with her scholarship to help with her room and board. She sold her meal voucher for a hundred bucks and handed it over to Leroy with instructions to get as many pills as he could. She could deal with no food, but as this point she couldn't deal without the drugs.

And then one day, he hadn't been able to find her any, and she collapsed on the locker room floor in full withdrawal.

When Coach West had found her, she hadn't been able to tell him the truth. She had blamed the breakdown on lack of sleep and stress over finals. It had her hurt to be untruthful, but Naomi was proud and she couldn't bear to lose the respect of the one person who believed in her. Instead, she had lied to him.

Chapter 20

The next morning, Macy's mother gave her daughter her very first lesson in cooking. She smiled at Macy as she showed her the proper technique to crack an egg on the rim of a ceramic bowl as if it were rocket science. They made fried eggs, pancakes, and homemade hot chocolate.

Macy smiled to herself for no reason at all. She loved how easy it was to just hang out with her mother. It was like finding a real best friend.

Sweet and optimistic, her mother was infectious, and Macy hoped some of those good vibes might rub off on her.

Macy's mom looked up at the clock as she picked up her breakfast plate and put it in the sink. Macy was still bent over her plate like someone who hadn't eaten in a week. Something about being in the cold mountain air had certainly helped her appetite.

She dunked the rest of her bagel in her egg yolk. "I usually don't eat like this."

Her mother smiled. "Take your time, sweetheart. Enjoy. I just have to excuse myself. It's art time, and I better go open the sunroom for the children."

At that moment, there was a quick knock on the door and Conner ducked his head in. "Good morning, ladies!"

Macy pulled her bathrobe around her, suddenly aware of how thin her nightgown was. How she managed to be dressed for bed every time she ran into this man must be some kind of cosmic joke!

"Morning," Macy said self-consciously. She waved half-heartedly in his direction and ran her hand through her hair.

Conner ushered the chattering group of children through the door and onward to the art room.

One dark-haired, sullen girl hung back reluctantly and didn't remove her coat. Macy watched Conner come back to talk to her.

He bent down.

The angry young girl with her mouth drawn tight in a firm line was shaking her head. But Conner must have convinced her, because she reluctantly took off her coat and hung it up, then followed him in to join the other kids.

Macy got dressed and joined them all in the art room fifteen minutes later. She was freshly showered and elegant in a simple black linen dress.

Macy looked around the room at the joyful scene, and stopped when she caught Conner observing her carefully; he smiled at her transformation.

Blood rushed to Macy's cheeks. Good grief, this guy was so handsome, and he was looking at her so intently like he could see right through her. His masculine chiseled face and out of control broad shoulders made her weak. He was standing next to the dark haired girl who was absorbed in her painting.

He waved Macy over and introduced them. "Regina, this is Macy. She's Ms. Kennedy's daughter."

Regina raised her dark eyebrows and looked Macy up and down like she was her superior, though she stood barely five feet tall. Macy must've passed, because the girl finally stuck out her hand and looked her in the eye.

"Hi. How come we've never seen you before?"

Macy's mouth went dry. It was like a punch in the gut. Conner cleared his throat and Macy's heart beat a bit too fast.

"Do you paint?" Conner asked.

"Me?" Macy laughed. "Oh, no. I'm a lawyer – well, I will be when I pass the bar. I'll be joining my father's law firm. I really haven't had time to do anything else but study... but painting sure looks like fun."

Macy thought back to her freshman year in college when she had the nerve to consider a Bachelor of Arts degree in Art. All the classes available in sculpting, painting, and dance seemed so interesting it made her bubble up inside.

Macy looked at the children laughing and painting while they mixed bright colors and brushed their imagination into reality.

As if reading her mind, Conner said, "Well, you can't be an observer. Not when your mom is one of the best art teachers in Kissing Bridge!" With that, he took Macy squarely by the shoulders and gently maneuvered her over to the easel that was open right next to Regina.

Regina was in the midst of painting an incredible likeness of the still life that was on the table. It was vibrant and strong, like Regina herself.

Macy was impressed.

"Wow, that's really good."

Regina didn't break her concentration. Macy had to smile at her tough girl attitude. Conner leaned over. "Hey, Regina, maybe you could give our new friend here a lesson?"

Regina grunted.

Regina put down her brush and stepped back to consider her painting. She studied it for a moment, then suddenly dipped her paint into the black and made a big X straight through the whole painting.

Macy gasped. "It was so pretty! Why did you do that?"

"It doesn't matter if it's pretty. Art is messy because life is messy too." Regina glared at Macy with a challenging glint in her eye. "You got a perfect life or something?"

Macy was taken aback by the street savvy young girl who seemed to have about as bad an attitude as Macy herself.

Macy looked at her. "I've never been very good at art – my own father wouldn't even put my childhood art on the fridge, it was so bad." She laughed but it sounded hollow and sad even to her.

Regina put her hands on her hips. "It doesn't matter if you're any good at art. Didn't your mother tell you the drill? Don't you know this class is for the *losers*?" She jabbed her thumb at the two smaller children next to her playing with a Play-Doh sculpture. "We're the rejects. The kids that get bullied, parents are too busy, or they're just plain messed up..."

141

She stopped and mumbled. "Art is supposed to take you out of your real life, when things mess up outside, you still have...this." Regina looked at Macy and their eyes locked in understanding. Macy might not look it on the outside, and as an adult she had learned to stay composed, but she knew exactly how it felt to be unwanted, different and unlovable.

Regina put her paintbrush down and looked her in the eye.

"I'll help you."

Macy knew when a gauntlet had been thrown down. "Okay, little girl, you're on." Macy said, "But I'm warning you: I'm horrible at this and you may be wasting your time."

Linda West

Chapter 21

Samantha took a deep breath as she let herself into her old house. The bars on the window shook as she tried to gently close the door tight against the heavy winds blowing outside. She steeled herself for the berating that she knew was coming next.

"Goddammit, Samantha, do not bang the door shut!"

"Sorry, Dad," Samantha said quickly.

There was no use telling her father for the thousandth time that the door was broken and always slammed. He came around the corner and leaned up against the wall.

Officer Dwayne Myers was in his uniform and fingered his gun as he glared at Samantha as if she were a convict.

She had almost erased his anger-filled face from her memory, but seeing him again in all his viciousness evoked old paranoia and insecurities. He was a horrible big brute of a man, and despite her wealth of courage, she was still a third his size.

The whites of his eyes were almost completely red and bloodshot from drinking, and she could smell the liquor on his breath from across the room.

She drew herself up and tried to look casual as she turned and hung up her coat and scarf. You were supposed to be home taking care of your brother and sister," barked her father. "Where you been?"

Samantha pointed at her stage makeup and braided hair still in place from the play. "We had the finale of the show tonight...I told you days ago that I would be busy."

Her father slurred his words. "Oh, you been busy? Miss star of the show is too busy to take care of her brother and sister. Let me tell you something, little missy. If Tommy misses school one more day, you're out of acting class next semester."

Sam's eyes went wide. How dare he threaten to take away the only thing in her young world that brought solace and joy? She clenched her fists and sought for the correct response.

What would be her normal reaction? She certainly didn't want to give away that this time she wasn't going to be a victim. This time, everything was going to be different, very different.

"You can't hold me responsible for Tommy. Even if I go to school with him doesn't mean that he won't run out the door when we get there."

He pointed at her and narrowed his eyes. "Not my problem. *Your problem.* Take care of business or I'll lock you in the house every night to make sure that you do. Maybe leave Cujo outside to make sure you stay there. Understand?"

Sam felt the old pain rise up in spite of her new strength. Cujo was his German Shepard K-9 and he was trained to kill. Relatives were no exception.

She narrowed her eyes. Everything inside of her wanted to turn and defy him. She'd strangled back her words, binding them to herself to keep them in, all the while keeping a placid face. A practice she still used – only now it was to deal with her temperamental, narcissistic boss, Macy Kennedy.

Sam watched as her father grappled drunkenly in his pockets, searching for his squad car keys. She breathed a sigh of relief. He must have to get back to work.

From the other room, Samantha heard a sleepy little voice call her name. "Saaaam? Sam?"

It was Trulie, her two-year-old sister, most likely curled up in the living room in front of the TV. Far be it for her father to put the youngster to bed at a decent hour. Sam's heart leapt with love and protection for the toddler.

"It's me, Trulie," called Sam. "I'm coming." Samantha moved to go past her father who was blocking the doorway to the living room. As she tried to slip by, he reached out and yanked her hair hard.

"Ouch!" She yelped. She tried to free her long blonde braid from his meaty hand, but he wound it even tighter around his fist and used it to pull her in closer to his ugly face.

"You're getting too big for your britches, Sammy. That pretty face, just like your mom's…"

She avoided his eyes, and pulled back from him. After a long, tense beat, he released.

Sam took a deep breath and tried to remain calm. She realized that she still needed to be careful. Very careful.

Chapter 22

Sam lifted her baby sister into her arms. Some horrid CIA murder show banged out bullets on the TV. Samantha snapped it off. What an inappropriate thing for a young child to be watching before sleep.

She reached over and wrapped Trulie in her baby blanket. It was pink and furry and had a little bunny on it. Wherever Trulie went, the bunny blanket went with her.

The sweet little girl mumbled sleepily. "Sammm. Hungry."

Samantha groaned inside. Of course her father hadn't fed her.

Outside came the welcome sound of her father's patrol car driving away. It was safe to go back into the kitchen.

Sam carried Trulie into the kitchen, speaking in docile tones. "Okay, my sweetness, let's see what we can find for you to eat."

Trulie gurgled. "Sam. Hungry."

Samantha smiled. "I know, baby."

She opened the refrigerator. It was near empty as usual. Luckily Sam always kept some macaroni and cheese boxes hidden in her room for just such occasions. She had learned a long time ago not to count on food being in the house. Once she had started working, she had also started buying cheap canned goods at the Dollar General that she stashed away.

A flashback of their neighbors, the Tellmans, bringing Trulie home late one night made Sam's cheeks blaze in shame. Sam had been looking for her sister frantically when Mrs. Tellman showed up at the door with Trulie in tow. Trulie had crawled through their pet door, eaten their dog's food, and fallen asleep on the floor next to the bowl, still clutching her baby blanket.

Her brother, Tommy, came out of the back room just then and glanced around the kitchen fearfully, making sure his father was gone.

He had a miserable look on his young freckled face and big black and blue whelps on his arms. Her father was a pro at leaving marks that could be easily covered with clothes.

Tommy's eyes were red and swollen from crying and he was trembling. The house was cold as usual; her father threatened to beat them if they put the heat on when he wasn't home.

Samantha wondered what had happened *this time* to warrant her father's reason for this outrageous abuse. Could be anything. She'd seen him hit her brother for literally breathing too loud. Sadly, and luckily, her eight-year-old brother had grown up fast and gotten tough over the years.

"I'm going to make some food – are you hungry?" Sam said lightly.

Tommy nodded.

Sam wrapped her free arm around the shivering young boy of eight and ruffled his red hair so like their mother's. "It's going to get better, Tommy. Really."

He looked up at her with broken eyes and said nothing.

She had promised him that before, and they both knew she was lying. Life at that house would never get better, that's why Samantha was running away in four days.

Only this time, she was taking the children with her.

Chapter 23

Christmas 1998
A week before Christmas

Naomi woke in pain. Everything in her hurt and she wanted to scream, but her body felt dull and weak and she was unable to move.

Everything was black. She didn't know where she was. Naomi reached out her hands and touched the cold tile. She blinked open her eyes wide and took in her surroundings. She knew this place. It was the girl's gym locker room at UCLA.

Naomi's mind flew from one thought to the next. Did someone cut in a psychedelic with her pills, was she dreaming–was she dead?! She ruled out the last two. Too much bodily pain for that. It was as if every muscle screamed at high pitch.

A flash of a garish, overly decorated home, full moon, and a magical cookie scrambled up and made no logic in her mind as she lay on the cold floor.

She must be dreaming because she'd been dwelling on it just before she fell asleep, but it appeared that she was back to the exact moment in time when she had collapsed from withdrawals after practice, and...the pain, oh the agony! She moaned at the wrath of it.

Suddenly, her beloved friend and mentor Coach West was leaning over her with a concerned look in his eyes. His kind face and sincere expression made her heart catch. Coach West. The one truly good person she had ever known.

"Naomi, are you are all right?" His voice warbled above her, and she fought to focus.

Naomi's head felt woozy, and her body felt limp and weak.

She instinctively tried to sit up as if nothing was wrong but collapsed back to the floor.

"Whoa, there," Coach West said. He motioned for one of her teammates to bring her some water. Then he checked her pulse and urged her not to move. "Breathe, Naomi. Slow. That's a girl...easy does it...slow, deep breaths."

Naomi inhaled deeply and felt herself revive. She focused her eyes on Coach West; he was a broad shouldered, coffee skinned man with clear blue eyes. He held up a cup of water and helped her drink. His face was filled with worry and he had his Motorola flip phone open. "I'm going to call 9-1-1."

Naomi blinked back into her body. *Oh my gosh,* she thought, *am I really back in time? Even in a dream this is unbelievable.*

It was all starting to seem familiar. It was a week before Christmas.

The last day before holiday break. Her whole life she had wondered what her future would have held if she just had the guts to ask for help that day when she needed it.

Now she had that chance.

Coach West was checking her pulse and looking at her with a worried frown. He knew that a kid from the streets like Naomi didn't trust anybody, but sometimes in your life you need to trust someone.

"I know something's wrong, Naomi. Your teachers tell me your grades are slipping; they're worried about your scholarship. You have to maintain at least a C. That didn't used to be a problem. I know the accident threw you, but is there something else going on?"

Naomi looked up at her coach. Last time she had lied to him. This time, she wouldn't. Tears filled her eyes. Her chance was now.

"Coach, I think I'm going through withdrawals," Naomi confessed. "I started getting pain meds on the street because the doctor cut me off... I think it's gotten out of control."

The whole sordid truth came tumbling from her mouth.

A flicker of surprise and sadness registered on Coach West's face, and then he nodded. He picked up her hand and found her gaze. "You and me, we're going to fix this. Trust me?"

Naomi nodded.

"I'm going to take you to the hospital and we are going to find a way to handle this safely. Then we're going to get you through this together. You're not alone, Naomi."

Chapter 24

Light and joyful tittering filled the art room. The children discussed the big tree-lighting ceremony that was supposedly a huge event in Kissing Bridge.

Macy was attempting to paint the still life, but the paint was mostly all over her. Regina stopped her own painting and looked over at her student. Macy turned to her for confirmation. Regina shook her head.

"I told you!" Macy threw her hands up in frustration.

Regina pointed at her work. "You're too tight. Loosen up with your brush–it's free."

Macy laughed in spite of herself.

"Well, if you have faith in me, then I guess I'll keep trying…" She looked at her picture; it was ridiculously amateurish. Macy let out a big sigh. She jumped when she heard Conner's deep voice come from behind her.

"Your mother is an incredibly talented artist. I'm pretty sure she passed some of those genes on to you, along with those beautiful brown eyes."

Macy froze with her paintbrush dipped in the red acrylic. A rush of warmth ran through her. She focused on her painting as if it were the most important thing in her life. Anything was better than for her to make a fool of herself fawning over the proximity of Conner's gorgeous body near hers. The last thing she needed was for the small town hunk to think she was falling for him. He probably had a girl on every street corner in Kissing Bridge. Not that there were many street corners from what she'd seen.

Conner grabbed both of her shoulders in a supportive, coaching kind of way and said, "Don't give up, Macy."

She turned slowly to face him but he was already across the room, putting on his coat and boots.

"I'll be back to get the kids at the usual time, Mrs. Kennedy."

Macy's mom stopped helping one of the smaller children and looked up and waved goodbye to Conner.

"Thanks so much, Conner. I really appreciate you driving them over here, especially in this weather."

Conner waved from the door. "No problem, Mrs. K. Wouldn't miss it for the world. Have fun, kids."

Macy's eyes illuminated with an idea and she put down her brush and hurried to the door. Conner looked up, surprised. "I guess I'll be seeing you around."

Macy gulped.

His beautiful face this close up was unnerving. The only cleft manly-man chin she'd ever seen like his was in some Ralph Lauren commercial. Most of her boyfriends had been metrosexual men that had better manicurists than she did.

Macy had a mission, so she pushed all the thoughts of Conner's gorgeous self out of her mind.

"Hey, Conner, maybe you can help me with something?"

Chapter 25

Conner and Macy drove through the mountains of Kissing Bridge. Macy looked out the window and had to admit it was a beautiful small town. Of course, they were behind the times–literally now– but it was 1995, and still no one in this town even had a cell phone.

At first, when she couldn't get any reception, she had panicked. Clients, deadlines, jury selection, and then remembered she *actually was* in another time!

This was before she had taken the bar and became one of the fiercest defense lawyers in Manhattan. Right now, she just had her mom to think of. And that included making this the best Christmas ever.

Holiday songs blared from Conner's truck radio and he insisted on singing along. He slaughtered the Johnny Mathis' song, but Macy had to smile at his lack of giving a hoot.

Soon they arrived at the main street and Conner pulled off into the quaint Kissing Bridge Mountain town square. She could already see an open space in the center filled with people and surrounded by booths of Christmas goods for sale. A large Christmas tree highlighted the center and it dripped with ornaments and sparkling lights.

Macy leaned back in the seat. Conner looked over at her from underneath his dark lashes. She spotted a dimple appearing on the side of his face.

"What?" she said.

Conner looked at her. "Would you like to tell me what we're doing here?"

"My mom..." Macy shook her head. "She has hardly any Christmas decorations; you can barely tell it's Christmas at her house." Macy looked out the window.

They had both lost Christmas it seemed, for way too long.

She forced a smile on her face and turned to look at the hunk beside her.

"And since I have no idea what kind of decorations to buy for Christmas, I need your help!"

"You need *my help*?" Conner said with a smirk. Macy looked at him challenging her.

"Yes, you don't want to leave me alone. If I have it my way, all the Christmas decorations will be black with hints of silver like I saw on the cover of Vogue."

Conner put his hands up.

"No threatening. I'll help you."

They made their way to the jaunty holiday square, just down the short snowy walk. The street was alive with activity and Christmas cheer.

Macy was tiptoeing slowly along, barely able to traverse at all in her dangerously high-heeled black shoes, and she shivered in her slim black blazer.

Conner raised an eyebrow at her attire. "You don't have a coat or boots?"

Macy was irritated, and cold, and unable to walk.

"It's a Chanel jacket. I'm fine."

"Well you look kinda cold. I'm just saying, it's not very appropriate for the weather." He wiped snow off her shoulder.

The ice had already made a wet splotch on the thin fabric.

Macy opened her mouth in indignation. "When is Chanel not appropriate? That's the purpose of spending a lot of money on Chanel, *it's always appropriate*!"

Conner laughed. "Seriously, you don't have anything warmer to put on?"

Macy frowned. "Do you see me hiding a parka and boots someplace?"

Conner pointed to her huge purse. "Well I thought you might have them in your suitcase, but I didn't think it was polite to question a woman's dress – or lack thereof in your case."

Macy pulled her black Chanel blazer closer over her black linen dress and trudged along with a pout on her face. "It's not a suitcase, it's a Chanel bag limited edition, I might add."

Conner looked over at it. "Too bad you can't wear it."

Macy sulked. "I guess I'll add decent clothes for this impossible weather to my shopping list today."

Conner shook his head playfully and took off his big, tan coat and draped it around her.

In other times, Macy might have refused his kindness, out of pride, or more likely stubbornness. But right now she was too cold to be cool.

"Thanks," she said sincerely.

"My pleasure," Conner said. He had on a thick flannel red shirt and looked like he had jumped out of some lumberjack romance novelette. His gray eyes sparkled as he looked down at her expensive but useless footwear.

"We'll work on those shoes next, what do you say?"

Macy looked down at her gloriously expensive designer high heels now covered with snow and bits of muddy ice. Her feet were already wet all the way through as water seeped into the low cut sides.

"Let me guess – Chanel?"

Macy glowered at him.

He shook his head, then scooped her up and whisked her off her feet and cradled her in his arms. He strode purposely toward a corner booth that had a sign that said *Ski Wear.*

Before Macy could argue, Conner had plunked her down on the other side of the booth right next to an old gentleman that had laughing eyes and bifocal glasses.

"What have we got here, Conner?" The old gent dressed in overalls and plaid flannel looked Macy over curiously.

"Very serious, Flanagan. A woman in need of snow boots."

The old man lifted his glasses and peered down at Macy's expensive high heels. "Hmmm. I see the problem, and I think I can be of help."

He slapped Conner on the back good-naturedly and steered them toward the boot area. Before long, Macy had her Chanel high heels in her purse and new warm snow boots on her feet.

They strolled around and looked at the various shops with homemade presents and fresh baked Christmas goodies. The center was alive with holiday hopefulness and happy shoppers.

Conner looked over at Macy who was walking fine now that she had the proper footwear. "Not quite New York City."

"No not quite." Macy smiled as a sleigh passed drawn by four white horses dressed with mock reindeer ears.

Little children were in line to sit on Santa's lap and their parents smiled and chatted with each other as they waited. She was sure half the town was in attendance despite the frigid weather, and they all seemed to know each other.

They waved and greeted Conner as they walked by.

"Howdy, Conner; say hello to your father for me."

"Will do, Mr. Smith. And a hello to Mrs. Smith."

"Well, hello, Conner! No kids today?"

Conner laughed warmly. "They gave me a day off, Jack."

Macy couldn't help but be enamored by the easygoing energy between all the people.

"Is the entire population of Kissing Bridge in the center right now?"

Conner smiled and cocked his head. "Well, it's tree lighting day, so in short – yes." He laughed, deep and warm. "It's tradition. The official lighting of the Christmas tree is one of the most fun events in Kissing Bridge, not to mention all the cafés and food shops in town are giving away free samples."

Macy was aghast. "FREE? How do they make money giving away free things?"

Conner groaned amicably. "It's not about the money, Macy. It's about the spirit of Christmas."

Macy's face was still screwed up in amazement. She could only have imagined her father here, and she had to suppress a giggle.

Free samples.

Macy sighed and nodded her head. "Sounds great."

One booth caught Macy's attention; they sold blow-up lawn decorations for the holidays, and they had a huge inflated Santa on display.

"So where do we start?" Conner said.

Macy pointed at the booth and tugged Conner along toward it.

"Well, I was thinking ornaments for the tree and some decorations for the house, and as much as I hate to say it, maybe that big blow-up Santa for the lawn so it looks happy when you come in. The yard just seems so barren like something is missing..."

Conner raised his brows. "And you've decided that something is a two-story enormous blow-up Santa?"

Macy nodded. "Come on; let's grab it before somebody beats us to it!"

Conner whistled. "Okay, I guess I can tie it down to the back of the truck, but you're banned from anything else bigger than a fridge after this. Deal?"

"Deal," Macy said, laughing.

They procured the blow-up Santa, which the shop offered to hold until they were ready to load it, thankfully. Next they stopped at one booth selling Christmas lights.

Conner lifted up a strand of lights that dripped like icicles and glimmered. "What do you think about these for the outside of the house?"

Macy beamed. "They're amazing!! I mean, they're so totally holiday gaudy that they're actually beautiful."

Conner looked confused. "So that means you like them?"

Macy nodded. "Let's just say they're perfect for my mom's house."

She turned to the next booth and grinned. "Oh Conner, look at these ornaments. They're so special!" The girl behind the counter smiled back, rubbing her hands together to warm them.

"Yeah, the kids made them over at Mrs. Kennedy's art shop," the girl said.

Macy blinked. "You mean Lenora Kennedy? That's my mom." Pride welled in her chest. "They're perfect; I'll take 100 of them."

The girl froze. "I'm not sure if we have that many." She turned to look at the display. "But boy is my Girl Scout captain going to be happy when she finds out we sold so many of these ornaments! We donate everything to the church services."

Conner wrapped one of his arms around Macy's shoulder casually and smiled at her.

"Well done. The best decorations Kissing Bridge has to offer and a charitable contribution all in one!"

Macy beamed up at him. His arm around her felt so comforting and right.

Conner was already laden down with bags but Macy was still shopping as she pointed excitedly to one shop after another selling Christmas delights.

Soon he looked at her and chided, "I think we've bought something from every store. Are we missing anything?"

She looked up at him with a smirk. "Well I did have my eye on that lovely Douglas Fir Christmas tree over at the Green Elves Santa Shop."

Conner laughed at her and said, "Of course you did."

Macy shrugged. "I mean, we need a place to put all those ornaments I just bought!

Conner's grey flannel eyes sparkled with mischief. "I think Kissing Bridge might be rubbing off on you, Macy Kennedy."

Chapter 26

Conner had gone back to the parking lot to deposit all their bags into his truck, and Macy was sipping a hot chocolate enjoying the small town kinship as she waited for him.

The choir began singing "Hark the Herald Angels Sing", and Macy felt her heart lurch. The carolers were all dressed in green and gold and three smaller children had bells which they rang in accompaniment. Macy couldn't help but smile from ear to ear. Christmas in Kissing Bridge was beautiful and kind of magical too.

Sure, they had chic decorative style sense in Manhattan, but this was different. Everywhere she looked, there were families, lovers, and children smiling with the anticipation of Christmas.

Macy spotted a booth that said *Unique Christmas Present Ideas.* That sounded intriguing. She wanted to buy a gift for her mother. She wasn't sure what she liked, and she didn't seem to be at all materialistic.

Macy moved closer to the sign and saw that it was a pet adoption booth. Inside people played with puppies and kittens. Macy looked in with trepidation. She was not an animal person, not that she was a people person either. Still she wasn't sure which scared her more.

She peeked over the edge of the booth and smiled at the antics of some kittens playing with a big ball of yarn. Two of them were tangled up in it and one had it wrapped around his tail. A little girl was on the floor gently trying to untangle them as they all rolled around, joyfully wrapping themselves up even more.

The teenaged girl behind the cash register called out to Macy. "You can come in – we encourage touching the product! She smiled at her, and coaxed her more. "Only some of them bite."

Macy looked up at her inquisitively, not getting the joke, and lightened up. She let herself inside and immediately a little brown puppy ran up to her. Macy bent down to pet it and it peed on her new boots.

"Oh my–" The girl came over and picked up the puppy. "Sorry about that; he's still a puppy. Good thing you're wearing water repellent snow boots."

Macy looked down at her wet boot. That was an understatement.

The girl handed Macy a couple paper towels to wipe off her boot. Macy dropped the used towels in the garbage by the Christmas tree in the corner of the booth. As she moved to walk away, a little furry paw stuck out from the pine tree branches and swiped at her.

Macy looked down, but there was nothing there.

She bent over and peered through the branches at the bottom.

Macy spotted a tiny pair of yellow ears hiding behind the Christmas tree. She bent down to see the kitty, and he ducked his head back, scared. Macy sat down and drummed her fingers on the floor; the little tabby stretched out a tiny striped yellow paw and grabbed her finger, then disappeared. Macy giggled. She continued to play the game with the cautious kitty, until one of the girls came over.

"I see you've found our little shy guy."

Macy looked up and tucked a strand of hair behind her ear. "Well, officially just his paw and ear, but he sure is cute."

The girl winked. "Hold on, I have the cure."

She returned with a little catnip treat and gave it to Macy. "Try this."

Macy held the treat out to the hiding kitty.

Slowly, he emerged from his hiding place and crept. With soft fur around his lips, he nibbled on the treat. Then he looked up at Macy expectantly. She threw her hands up. "All out, kitty, sorry." The cat looked at her longer. Macy felt sorry for him; he seemed so scared and small and scrawny.

"What's wrong with him?" Macy asked.

"Ahh, poor thing. He was the runt and he got picked on all the time, so now he hides. He's so shy, nobody thinks of taking him home. All of his sisters and brothers got adopted ages ago, but we still have this little guy."

Macy looked at the cat nobody wanted. She felt like the human version.

"I'll take him."

Macy paid for the kitten and the girl waved goodbye to them. "Best of luck with Toulouse."

Macy froze and looked down at the tiny tiger paw sticking out of the hole in the box she held.

"Toulouse?" She said in awe.

The girl caught Macy's expression. "Yeah, we named him after the painter Toulouse-Lautrec. If you don't like it, you can change it."

Macy looked back at the box. "No," she said with a smile tugging at the side of her mouth. "My mother is an artist. I couldn't have picked a better name myself."

Macy was holding a big cardboard box with a furry striped tail sticking out of one of the holes on the side when Conner caught up with her again.

"I just thought I should run some things back to the truck."

He eyed the box with the rumbling inside.

"Because I thought I might need to carry more things," he finished. "Hand it over."

Macy handed Toulouse over to Conner and he threw his head back in exasperation. "I see you found the pet adoption."

Macy nodded as she handed the box with the kitten over to Conner's sure hands.

"Hey, what's going on there?" Macy questioned as she saw a crowd of people around a group of end booths and a judges' stand with a scoreboard being erected.

Conner smiled. "Oh, very important stuff going on there. Tomorrow on Christmas Eve they hold the annual cookie contest and it's quite a competition. You won't want to miss that."

They wandered closer to the busy area. Contest contenders were busy decorating their booths and giving out free samples as they prepared for tomorrow's big event.

There was one delightful booth decorated all in Tiffany blue that was very stylish, and it was jam-packed with people. Macy nudged through the crowd to see what the fuss was about, and then stopped dead in her snow boots as she read the sign on the booth – THE LANDERS SISTERS.

She pulled back and closer to Conner. He beamed and his entire face smiled big white teeth as he pointed at the popular booth.

"You're going to have to try some of the Landers sisters' cookies; they are the best in Vermont!"

Macy raised her eyebrows. "Not Carol?"

Conner nodded. "You know them! Yes, Carol and Ethel Landers
are famous here in Kissing Bridge for their baked goods. I'm sure you'll meet them; they're very close friends of your mom's." He nudged Macy good-naturedly. "Plus, it's hard not to miss Carol with that big beehive of hers that sticks out in every crowd."

Suddenly Macy spotted Carol herself, behind the booth. Carol tilted her flaming red beehive to the side, like an antenna trying to get reception, as her blue eyes scanned the crowd like a lighthouse searching through the sea of people.

Macy sucked her breath in and backed up quickly, ducking behind Conner to hide. "Ahh Conner shouldn't we get the kitty home and out of that box?"

"Good idea," he said as he turned and scrutinized her crouching down behind his back.

She linked her arm through his and pulled him toward the exit, away from the senior's eagle, knowing gaze. Still, out of the corner of her eye, Macy could have sworn she caught Aunt Carol wink at her from her booth.

Macy groaned inwardly. How did Carol Landers end up in her dream?

Obviously Macy had no control.

CHAPTER 27

Tonight was the night. It was Christmas Eve. Samantha locked the door and watched her father's patrol car pull away once more. She drew in a deep breath. Her dad was on his way to work, and she was to meet Riley in an hour.

That gave her more than enough time to pack up Tommy's and Trulie's things.

Trulie was in the living room playing with Tommy's hair as he stared dully at Rudolph the Red Nose Reindeer on the TV. He had a fresh black eye. Sam looked at him and opened her mouth to ask, but snapped it shut. Her father knew they were on vacation, so the proof of his abuse would be faded into oblivion by the time Tommy went back to school.

She looked at Tommy with her heart in her eyes, bent down and held his hands. He looked so young and so streetwise all at once.

"I'm going to get us out of this," she whispered. He ignored her and stared straight at the TV as if in a trance.

Sam looked out through the window to make sure the road was clear, then she darted up the stairs to their rooms.

She had already arranged all the clothes she had to pack in one place. All she had to do was grab them and put them in the extra suitcase she had picked out of the dumpster the other day. It smelled, but she had washed it in the shower and dried it with her blow dryer when her father was at work.

She looked out the top window of the attic, scanning the snowy streets again for any sign of danger. Even if her father was gone, there were still gossips in the neighborhood, and she couldn't take any chance.

Time to make her move.

She grabbed her school satchel, dumped it out, and pushed the contents under the bed she shared with Trulie.

Within moments, she had Tommy's and Trulie's things stuffed into the extra suitcase.

Time to get the money.

The last time she had tried to hide her getaway money, her father had found it. This time she had been smarter.

She had left a couple dollars in the bible bank she had hollowed out for bait, but she had hid away the rest of her small bounty on the back plate of the family photo frame she always kept by her bed. Last time she had taken the photo as a reminder of her brother and sister.

This time she was taking them and the money instead.

She grabbed the old photo frame and ripped off the back cardboard to expose her cash.

Sam gasped.

She pulled the frame apart, tearing out the photo and tossing it on the ground followed by the backing.

Nothing.

An eerie coldness crept up the back of her spine, causing her neck hairs to stand up.

The money was gone.

Her father had found it – *again.*

Sam's head spun. She needed money. How was she going to take care of food and things for the kids? And if her father had found the money again, despite her changing things, what else might still occur that she didn't plan for?

She looked out the window again, afraid of seeing the telltale car lights of her father's return.

She had to go.

She had no choice. And the kids, they had to come too.

But what about the money? Riley and his trust fund.

He'd said they'd be fine on it until they got work as actors. Certainly there was a little extra to feed two small children? They wouldn't need a bigger place; the kids could just sleep on the couch. It would be rough for a minute, but they'd make it.

Riley loved her, and he was great with her sister and brother. He had always brought them treats and played video games with Tommy when her father wasn't around. No, it wouldn't be easy with the kids along, but they'd make it.

She looked at the clock. 6:15. Time to go.

She strapped on her backpack, picked up the suitcase, and headed down the stairs from the attic.

"Tommy!" She called downstairs. "Can you put Trulie in her snow clothes please?"

Silence answered her as she dragged the bag down the stairs, *bump, bump, bump.* She came into the living room and snapped off the TV and looked around.

Trulie was on the couch in her footie pajamas wrapped in her pink blanket. But Tommy was gone.

Chapter 28

Sam desperately called every phone number belonging to Tommy's friends she could find, but no one had seen him. It was Christmas Eve; everyone had their minds on happier things.

Sweat trickled down her forehead despite the cold temperature. Tommy still hadn't come home, and it was nearing the time they had to meet Riley. Her father got out of work at 8:00 and it was 6:30 now.

Riley was picking her up at 6:45, and it was a fifteen-minute walk in good weather. Sam looked outside at the inclement weather and shivered. It was now or never.

She picked up the baby and suitcase and shut the door of her old life behind her. Samantha hurried down the snow filled sidewalk, casting furtive glances back and forth, looking for her brother. She stopped at the garage and grabbed Trulie's car seat and shut the door quietly, all the while keeping one eye on the street.

She crept down the snowy walk, barely able to keep a hold of Trulie and the seat as she dragged the suitcase along behind them toward the meeting place. The walk was slippery and Sam stopped to reposition her backpack.

The door to her neighbors, the Davenports, suddenly bolted open, spilling festive music along with Mrs. Davenport into the street, herding her young daughter ahead of her. She spotted Samantha and stopped dead in her tracks.

"Samantha, what are you doing out with...?" She took in the luggage and car seat.

"Hi." Gosh darn it, Sam was not happy to see her. Mr. Davenport worked on the force too. "Hey," said Sam, "have you seen Tommy? We have an...event to go to."

Mrs. Davenport didn't seem to believe her for a second.

"No, we haven't seen Tommy today at all. Is everything all right?"

"Yes." The lie came so easy. "My friend is having a big party – lots of food – well, it's Christmas Eve but...anyway, I know Tommy would love to go."

Mrs. Davenport looked down at the suitcase, the baby seat, and Trulie bundled in Sam's arms.

"I was just running to pick up my niece," Mrs. Davenport said. "Why don't I drop you off?"

Sam held her breath.

Mrs. Davenport drove them in silence. Samantha checked her watch. It was 6:40. Riley would be at their meeting place in five minutes. She darted her eyes around the streets, estimating the time. At least five minutes to get there, even driving.

That was when she spotted her brother's telltale red carrot top head. He was playing snowballs with a group of boys near the parking lot of the high school.

"Stop!" Sam cried. "This is great, Mrs. Davenport, thank you. There's Tommy...

the party is just around the corner; he must have gone ahead of us."

Mrs. Davenport looked like she didn't believe her, but for once Samantha didn't' care.

She unhooked Trulie and her baby seat and grabbed her suitcase from the back. "Merry Christmas. See you tomorrow." Sam shut the door.

It was cold out, and Trulie started crying. "Cold, Sam, cold."

Sam hugged her tight as she struggled to pull the baby seat, luggage, and Trulie through the snow.

She called out to Tommy, but he ignored her and ran away laughing with his friends "Tommy!" she screamed again. "Please…"

She wanted to cry, she wanted to fall in the snow and give up.

She looked at the beautiful Christmas scene displayed on the front lawn of her high school and it seemed to mock her.

Sam tucked Trulie and her blanket into the car seat and belted her in.

She looked up and down the road. It was clear. She scrambled up onto the platform with the Christmas diorama and climbed on the reindeer, unfastening the piece of rope that attached the faux reins to the fake Santa sleigh on display.

She leapt down with the rope and fumbled with her cold hands to fasten it to the baby car seat. She shouldered her backpack on again, took the luggage in one hand, and dragged the rope attached to the makeshift sled with her baby sister and started off in search of Tommy.

Chapter 29

Naomi looked around the white walls of the strange room. The rehab in Six Pines Valley was nothing fancy. It wasn't like one of those upscale Malibu beachfront addiction centers for rich people who got massages all day and one-on-one counseling by Harvard psychologists. No, this was the budget rehab.

It felt more like a prison with the bars on the window and the strict rules. No phones. No contact. No drugs.

The bare-bones center suited her though. Naomi would have felt self-conscious in some fanc. Somehow Coach

West had gotten her into this facility, and she felt blessed.

The rehabilitation program lasted thirty days, which also spanned the holiday vacation at college. If she just stuck to the program and stayed sober, she had her entire life in front of her yet.

She was in a small private hospital facility within the rehab where they were overseeing her detox. Coming off of pain pills proved more painful than the original pain she had been fleeing. Another irony of life.

She winced as she felt the wet sheets beneath her. She was sweating profusely. Her whole body felt wet and sticky with the toxins pouring out of her. She gritted her teeth and sucked in a deep breath. She'd been through a lot in her life; she would get through this too. She had to.

She didn't know where the money had come from to get her into a rehab. God knows these kinds of places were only for upper class bank accounts. Even the cheap addiction centers were not cheap.

She thought back to the commercials she had seen on TV before, two rich white men standing in front of a multi-million dollar mansion. "Do you have a loved one that needs help? Come pay us more than most people's whole savings and we'll fix them up proper. Only takes one or ten times…"

She always wondered what type of people paid 100,000 dollars to go to one of those places where everything seemed to be erased with the badge of sobriety but they just came back to treatment a few months later. No one mentioned that part.

She suspected that Coach West had paid for it. Naomi clasped her hands together to thank God for giving her a second chance. She had abandoned her faith long ago, but she found herself praying earnestly now. "O Lord, let me really have this second chance. I promise I will do better…"

Even if this was only a dream, for a moment, Naomi loved herself again. And for that moment, she believed in herself again. For that one brief moment, her future looked bright instead of doomed.

Okay, she was in a rehab, but she'd been in worse situations before.

People had downs; it was the ups that mattered.

So she was down now, no doubt, very down, but when she got up again, she was going to make the Olympic team and show everybody what she was made of.

Chapter 30

Samantha was nearly out of strength. "Tommy!" she screamed. He ignored her and kept playing. "Tommy!" She yelled again urgently. "I need you to come with me." Silence. "Please, Tommy. Please."

Tommy stopped playing and walked over to his sister. His friends followed. He tried to appear cool and casual in front of the crew.

"What's up, sis?"

Sam picked herself up and wiped her eyes and stood tall.

"Time for us to go."

Tommy wasn't about to show any weakness or emotion to his tough buddies from the streets. "Go where?" he said harshly. "Leave me alone, Sam, I'm hanging with my friends. I'll catch you later." He turned to leave and Sam reached out and grabbed him.

"Tommy – I'm serious. We need to go."

Sam looked her younger brother in the eye, and Tommy knew something was different. He took in his baby sister asleep in the makeshift sled car seat and Sam with her backpack and a strange piece of luggage.

"Better go, Tommy," one of his buddies cooed in a baby voice. The others laughed.

Tommy's face went red and he gave Sam a nasty look.

"Go on. Like I said, I'll catch up with you later."

Tommy turned away from her and ran off again.

Samantha didn't know what to do. Riley was probably already waiting for her and each moment they were out on the street was dangerous.

She didn't trust Mrs. Davenport to stay quiet either.

Sam fell to her knees and brought both her hands to her face. Oh lord, she had tried so hard and was failing so badly. The sound of a dog barking sent shivers down her spine. For all she knew, her father was out looking for them with his killer dog right now.

Gosh darn it. She wasn't going to fail. Too many lives depended on it.

Sam rose up and she threw off her backpack. She walked over and snatched up Trulie from the car seat, leaving the luggage and seat behind, and stumbled after Tommy as quickly as she could through the deep snow.

She found him around the corner of the bushes. He was back with his cronies, smoking a cigarette, looking at her like he dared her to reproach him.

Sam was not going to stop. She approached the motley crew with Trulie in her arms.

"Tommy! Look please just believe me! Just once trust me okay? Please come with us."

Tommy's friends chuckled at her. Tommy blew a long hit of smoke out of his mouth. She wanted to snatch the cigarette right out of his hands and drag him behind her if she had to. She just didn't have the strength to force him.

Trulie awoke and smiled up at her big brother and stuck her little pink baby hands out to him.

"Tommy! Tommy!"

Her brother's name was one of the few words she could say.

The other boys chided him. "Better go babysit little mama."

Tommy gave them a withering look.

He looked at Samantha.

"Hand her over."

Samantha handed the baby to him and she immediately started gurgling happily and playing with his red hair.

"Tommy, Tommy!"

"Come on, then," he said to Samantha. "Let's get going."

Chapter 31

They gathered up the luggage and baby seat.

"You brought stuff for me?

Samantha nodded. "We're getting out of here Tommy. For real."

She hurried down the walk. "Hurry please!" She urged. Tommy followed huffing along behind her. "Where are we going?"

Sam brightened as the school auditorium came into view. She was supposed to meet Riley in the back by the casting door.

"California – where it's warm! Come on we're almost there. Riley's picking us up."

They lumbered to run the last hundred yards to the pick up spot. Tommy puffed out between breaths. "We're not going back home?"

"Nope never." Sam said happily.

She turned the corner and there he was.

Riley was parked in front of their designated spot in his red mustang. Sam smiled from ear to ear and waved to him.

Riley revved his engine and pulled the mustang up next to them. He rolled down the window and smiled his movie star grin.

"Sorry I'm late, babe. Ready to go to...?" His voice trailed off as he took in the kids and baby seat.

Riley ruffled his hands through his thick dark hair. "What are you doing with the baby? Are we dropping them off?" He glanced at Tommy, and Tommy cast his eyes to the ground.

Sam threw open the back door of the car. "Change of plans Riley. We have to take the kids I can't leave them."

Samantha handed Trulie to her brother to hold as she bent to fasten the car seat to the back seat of the mustang. She threw in the luggage and motioned for Tommy to get in.

Sam hopped in the front seat with a smile on her face. It had been rough, but they had done it. She had all three of them, safe and warm, and on their way to a life they would love.

She smiled at Riley, but he was staring at her blankly. From a distance Sam could hear the sound of dog barking again, and her skin froze at the thought of her father if he was to find them.

"Let's go." Sam said with urgency. "I don't trust my neighbors not to call my father and get every patrol car out looking for us."

But Riley didn't move. He just looked in the backseat at the sullen boy with the black eye and the little girl that was now fast asleep in her baby seat.

"What's wrong?" Sam said. "Let's go."

Riley looked at her and whispered. "Seriously you're kidding me Sammy right?"

Sam's eyebrows arched together in confusion.

"No I'm not kidding. Now Riley lets go!"

He continued to stare at her in a way she hadn't seen before. As if she suddenly had leprosy.

Trulie woke up and started crying. "Food...hungry."

Sam's heart lurched. She hadn't had a chance to feed her a proper dinner in the rush to leave. The poor baby was probably starving. Tommy ruffled her hair to play with her and calm her down.

"Tommy look in my bag I have some baby cookies." Sam said.

Riley threw his hands up in the air.

"Whoa what's going on here Sam?"

He turned off the car and looked at her with a pained expression.

"This... *they* weren't part of the plan. We can't take a bunch of kids to California. We need to be free agents and focus on our careers."

"Riley." Sam pleaded and took both his hands in hers. "It will be okay I promise. They won't be any problem...I can't..."

He looked at her sadly, and shook his head.

"Come on Riley please!" She was begging now. "They don't eat much and I know you have the extra money. We will figure it out I can't just leave them!"

She trailed off as Riley's eyes glazed over. He was looking at her as if she had sprouted a third hand out of her head.

"It's not gonna work Sammy. I'm not a family man. I didn't sign up to take care of a bunch of kids. If you want to do that then you do that. I'm going to go to California and be a movie star."

Sam dropped his hands. So much for love conquering all. She had never even considered that Riley wouldn't go along with her plan. He of all people knew what her father was like.

Sam lifted her chin. "I thought you loved me?"

Riley started the car again. What had seemed like safety just minutes before now seemed like an executioners' chair.

He cleared his throat. "Just tell me where to drop you guys off. Home?"

Sam looked at him with daggers shooting. "Home?"

She nearly spit it out.

"I'd rather die."

Samantha was in shock. She hadn't planned for Riley to not go along with her plan, and now they were all in danger. She looked out of the window of the car unable to move.

Tommy reached out his hand from behind the back seat and clutched Sam's shoulder in consolation. She turned and looked at him. He looked so young and yet so old. His black eye was now an ugly eggplant bruise that looked like it hurt.

"Let's go Sammy." He said in a whisper. "Like you said – we'll just get out of here. We don't need him."

Sam was frozen. She looked from the backseat, to Riley, and the unwelcoming outdoors.

Tommy got out of the car silently, and pulled the luggage out after him and threw it into the deep snow. He went to the other side and unhooked his baby sister and her chair, and carried them over and set them next to the luggage. He slammed the door shut, and came over and opened up Sam's passenger side door.

Tommy grabbed her backpack off the floor, and undid her seat belt for her, as if she were a child. He put the backpack on, and held out his hand to coax his sister out of the car.

Samantha stared straight ahead traumatized and immobile. The warm car and happy holiday music held her like glue to the front seat.

Tommy urged her gently. "Come on Sammy."

She finally looked at her brother, her sad green eyes meeting his matching ones, and she numbly moved her body out of the front seat.

She was barely out of the car before Riley hit the gas and roared away into the night in a flash of red.

Sam looked after their departing escape vehicle.

She had really screwed this one up.

Chapter 32

"You just can't go by the whims of your spirit, Mom," Macy said as she attempted to paint half-heartedly. "You can't ignore it either," her mother countered.

Echoes of surfer boy Thor and his *Spirit Voice* lectures came wafting back to Macy's mind. Maybe this is what he meant. There were other things than money and success. There was art and the calling of the soul, and connection with a higher power. Macy had learned all about money. But she had never learned to listen to her heart.

This clear Christmas Eve morning, her mother and she were making art and listening to happy holiday music. They both had big mugs of hot coffee and a plate of fresh cinnamon rolls between them.

Her mother clasped her hands together and looked closely at Macy's painting, but she didn't say anything. Macy stopped. "I'm horrible, aren't I?"

Her mother shook her head. "You're just learning; don't be so hard on yourself, honey. Come look at this."

Her mother led her to a piece of art that hung on the wall. It was full of life and emotion and color. It was stunning.

"This is Regina's."

Macy sucked in her breath. It was more than good.

"She's very talented," Macy said in appreciation.

Her mother nodded. "Yes, she is. But why?"

Macy shrugged. "In the genes, maybe? Practice?"

Her mother shook her head.

"No. It's good because it has *feeling* in it. And her feeling translates to the viewer so you feel too. That's the true key. Great art makes you feel."

Macy studied the piece. "She's so unhappy yet she's so gifted."

Her mother looked at her. "Sounds like someone else I know."

Macy looked up at her, then laughed despite herself. "I really am a mess, aren't I?"

Her mother hugged her. "Oh, darling that's life. One delightful mess. You really can't get it wrong if you follow your bliss."

Macy hugged her mom tight. "I'm so glad I came home, Mom."

Her mom tucked a piece of Macy's hair behind her ear affectionately. "Me too, sweetheart. More than you'll ever know."

They pulled away, and her mother wiped tears from her eyes. "Okay, now – let's get back to that picture of yours and see how we can get you to let your heart show with colors!"

She glanced at her mother's easel next to her and the sketch she had been working on. Mrs. Kennedy liked to do sketches of people doing ordinary things, slices of real life and the simplicities that filled people's days.

It was a picture of Macy at her easel, painting. Her mom had been sketching her all the while.

"Mom," Macy chastised. "I look horrible in this red Christmas sweater and – what are these?" She pointed to her baggy gray pants she was wearing.

"They're called sweatpants, darling, and they are exactly what you want to be wearing when you're creating; you certainly don't want to worry about messing up your clothes when you're working on a masterpiece."

Macy looked over at her painting. "I can assure you this will never be a masterpiece. But if you're going to sketch me *at least* let me put on something more elegant!" Macy laughed at herself and the thought of her bad holiday house outfit being forever immortalized in her mother's art.

Suddenly, Macy stopped short, when she heard a weird guttural sound.

Her mother suddenly winced and folded over, and clutched at the side of her chest.

"Mom!" Macy called out. "Are you all right?"

Her mother nodded and took a couple breaths as Macy ran toward her and bent down next to her. "Should I call a doctor?"

She shook her head. "No, no I'll be fine. I just had a little pain lately on this side. It goes away. I probably put away too many easels at one time..."

Macy was concerned. "Here, just take some deep breaths and let me get you something to drink."

She ran to the kitchen and got a glass of water from the sink. "Drink."

Her mother did as ordered and soon her pinched face relaxed and her breathing returned to normal.

Macy kneeled back down next to her and looked at her directly. "Mom, I'm concerned."

She waved her off. "Honey, it's fine. I'm strong as an ox."

She had on a brave face on, but Macy wasn't taking any chances. She moved to the house phone and picked it up.

"I'm going to call your doctor; I don't care if it is Christmas Eve."

"Darling, I'm fine, really."

"Mom, I insist. Now where do you keep your emergency numbers?"

Her mother looked up in chagrin.

"Macy–I don't have a doctor. I've never gone to the doctor. I eat well, I take care of myself, and I'm healthy. I don't need a doctor to tell me that. I just overexerted myself, I'm sure. The burden of cookie baking." She cracked a smile, but Macy didn't laugh.

"You've never seen a doctor? Mom, are you living in the Middle Ages? Do you need money? I have lots; we can go right now–"

"No, Macy, it's not about the money. I don't like doctors."

Macy bent down in front of the chair and took both her mother's hands as if she were the child.

"Mom, I know you live in this fantasy wonderland of art and spirit and it's beautiful, but you can't deny the real world and responsibilities."

Her mother looked up at her and Macy's heart skipped a beat at the look in her eye.

Macy hurried on anyway despite what she knew in her heart.

She wasn't going to the doctor, no matter what Macy said.

"It's Christmas Eve, so it's probably not the easiest time to get an appointment. But as soon as the holidays are over, I'm taking you to the doctor myself, I swear."

Macy stopped as she realized she would be gone by Christmas.

Or woken from this dream.

Either way, there wouldn't be *an after Christmas* for her and her mother.

Her mother reached out and touched Macy's face with a twinge of sadness in her eyes. "Let's just enjoy this special Christmas together."

Chapter 33

Sam pulled the makeshift sled with Trulie, and Tommy dragged the luggage nearly twice his size along beside her. Sam fought the tears that threatened to stream down. She had no idea what she was going to do. Now she was in a worse state than before.

She stiffened as a police car turned at the far corner and headed toward them. She watched the black and white drive into the athletic part of the school they had just left, as if looking for something.

Sam suddenly had the horrid feeling that Mrs. Davenport had called her father and told him about the odd interaction they'd had earlier.

She looked at her watch. It was past 8:00 p.m. and her father would have come home and noticed them missing by now.

Sam sucked in her breath and watched as the car turned on its top lights and they began to spin, lighting up bright patches in the snow.

"Hide!" Sammy screamed.

Tommy looked around and spotted what Sam had seen.

"Here!" He motioned. "These bushes have a hollow area in between."

Tommy ran into the clump of trees, warring against the high snow with his baby sister in his arms. Sam scooped up some snow and threw it over the luggage and car seat, then crawled in toward the protective cover of the bushes after him.

They huddled together in fear and to ward off the cold winds that were blowing sheets of snow. A search light beamed upon the area where they had left the luggage.

Sam bit her tongue.

The light hit the baby seat – partially uncovered by the snow falling off it – and

Sam prayed. After a long moment, the light swung in a different direction as they backed up farther into the protective limbs of the snowbush.

The light flashed around the area for a while, then snapped off.

Sam grabbed Tommy's free hand and they held their breaths and listened as the patrol car drove away.

Sam went out first, to make sure the coast was clear. She uncovered the baggage and waved for Tommy to follow.

They resumed trudging in the direction away from home. They had to get out of their neighborhood, at least, even if it meant walking. Too many people knew them and her father had some clout. She needed a new plan. Home was out. Friends too, obviously.

Still they had to get off of the sidewalk. It was too dangerous. The woods were up ahead. Sam battled with the options. Chance the tundra in the woods or her father's abuse if they got caught.

Tommy pulled the oversized suitcase behind him and it bumped along the ground behind him awkwardly. The snow was falling hard now, and all three of them were openly shivering from the exposure.

Sam decided they'd have to go through the woods. It was dangerous, but so were the streets. They were just approaching the trail, when a car came down the street slowly.

Sam sucked in her breath.

She glanced back quickly, confirming it wasn't a police car, or worse yet her father. She didn't recognize the car, but that didn't mean it wasn't one of her father's cronies out looking for them. At this point she didn't trust anyone.

The car slowed as it approached them.

Sam covered up Trulie with her blanket, and pulled Tommy into her closer. The car came to a full stop next to them, and a man rolled down the car window.

"Can I help you kids?"

Those kind blue eyes, that soft caring tone – Sam looked at the man behind the wheel. It was Harold!

Everything inside of her wanted to scream and grab her future husband and hug him and say, "Harold! Harold! Thank God you found us. I love you!"

But of course, he didn't know her. He was just some Good Samaritan being kind to some strangers on Christmas.

"Can I give you a ride…?" he said with concern. At the look in Samantha's big green eyes, his words stuck in his mouth. "Somewhere?"

He silently took in the sad situation, the trembling trio, and Tommy's black eye.

He cleared his throat.

"I know you don't know me, but it's Christmas and all, and it looks like you got caught in a bad situation. I'd like to help."

Samantha nodded gratefully. "Thank you, yes. Thank you Har–"

He looked at her oddly. "Have we met?"

Samantha shook her head.

His soft blue eyes flickered with a recognition he couldn't place.

Harold got out of the car and started loading their belongings into the back of his trunk. He expertly fastened the child seat and reached his hands up to Sam to hand him Trulie.

The tiny tot had frozen tears streaks down her little red cheeks and Harold's heart leapt as he buckled her in and covered her up with her pink baby blanket.

Samantha opened the door for Tommy and he hopped in the back.
Harold looked over at him. "You warm enough, Scout? I have another blanket I can grab."

Tommy shook his head. He was silent and sullen, but the inside of the car was warm and toasty.

After the kids were set. Samantha piled into the front passenger seat and let out a big sigh. *Thank you, God. Thank you for sending Harold.* He was the closest thing to an angel she had ever met. Sam's heart was bursting and she wanted to throw herself into his loving embrace.

Harold looked over at her. Why was this beautiful girl so hauntingly familiar, and what in the world was he going to do with this family that he had just picked up?

"Is there any place special you were heading that you want me to drop you off?" Harold asked in a kind voice.

Lights went off in Samantha's head. Good lord, she had nowhere to go, and Harold didn't know yet he'd fall in love with her. She had no idea what his life was currently like. All she knew for sure was that she could not go home, or let her father find them.

She considered telling Harold everything and throwing herself on his mercy, when he said,

"I was on my way to meet my fiancée…"

Samantha's heart fell. Of course, Harold was engaged to Estelle! It was 1995, and he had married her in 1996.

Sam's green eyes flashed like a hunted deer and she rattled her brain for an answer. Harold looked over and saw the look of desperation on her face as she glanced back at the children.

He cleared his throat. "As I said, I was just on the way to meet my fiancée at my parents' house for a big – and I mean BIG – Christmas Eve party. We all get together every year and with my family that always means a party. There will be lots and lots of food." He looked over at Tommy. "I bet you don't like turkey and stuffing and pies though, huh?"

Tommy's eyes went big. "I ain't eaten nothing since yesterday. I could eat your parents' house."

His genuine caring stirred Samantha's heart. She realized she would fall in love with Harold in any circumstance.

Food, warmth for the children. Her prayers had been answered – for the moment.

"Oh, except one thing…" He glanced at Sam and blushed in that adorable way he always did when he was embarrassed. "You're so pretty, I'm awfully sure my fiancée is not going to be too happy to see me walk in with you off the street. Not sure how to handle that."

"Maybe you can say we're old family friends?" Sam offered.

Harold nodded. "Maybe…still you might be too pretty for me to know at all." He laughed stiffly. "She's got a bit of a jealousy problem." He flipped the car back into drive. "Let's get going."

He drove down the pretty street with all the big houses decorated so gaily. Samantha looked out the window at the splendor as they rode deeper into the more affluent part of town and farther away from their own neighborhood.

Harold continued. "Don't get the wrong idea. Estelle is a great girl. Her dad is a dentist and they both think I'd be great in dental sales."

"You hate it!" Sam declared with a passion.

Harold turned to her again with a questioning expression. He pulled the car up a long drive toward the large country home on the hill ahead.

"*You'll*…hate it…." Sam amended.

"That's exactly what I said." Harold smiled. "Why do I feel like you know me so well and I just met you?"

Sam shrugged.

"I don't know," she said. *Maybe we're soulmates.*

Chapter 34

Naomi scratched her arm with fierceness.

She hurt all over. For the first few days, she barely knew where she. Now she yearned for that prior oblivion. She was angry one moment, screaming at the poor nurse, and reticent and weepy the next. She missed her easy out via pills.

Besides the yo-yo-ing of her emotional world, all her muscles seemed to dully ache at once.

She looked around the room. It was white with no decorations save the bed she was in and the machine with the hose attached to her arm. She watched the liquid drip into her. Hydrating her, she guessed. She closed her eyes and tried to shut out the pain, but the tears welled up again.

They flowed freely now as much from the detox pain as for regret for how wrong things had gone. But if God really had given her a second chance on this magical blue moon of Christmas, even if this was a dream, she was going to dream it better.

The nurse came in with a kind look on his face. He had dark eyes and a wide nose. "How are you feeling today, Naomi?"

Naomi gave a halfhearted smile. "Well, I'm not dead."

The nurse smiled back at her. "And I see you have your sense of humor back. So does that mean you're up for a visitor?"

Naomi's eyes widened. Who could be here to see her?

Before Naomi could ask who it was, Coach West appeared in the doorway. He was holding a large present with a big bow, and some silver bells jingled as he walked across the room and set the gift on the desk next to the hospital bed. There was kindness and concern in his blue eyes.

"How you doing, Naomi?"

"Better, Coach, really better."

He smiled. "Well, it's almost Christmas and I'm going away with my family for a few days, but I just wanted to make sure you were okay and that you had something to open up on Christmas morning."

Naomi straightened and looked at the present in surprise. "You got that for me, Coach?"

He smiled and the nurse left the room.

Naomi was taken aback. "You didn't have to do that..."

"I wanted to."

He went over the bed and took her hand in his. "Just get better, Naomi, promise?"

She looked him in the eye.

"I promise Coach. I will. "

He patted her hand and beamed at her. "I'm counting on it. We're gonna need our best runner to beat the Russian team this year."

Chapter 35

Samantha brought her hand to her heart. The Henderson's' home was the refuge she had prayed for. It was also a Christmas lover's delight.

A huge Christmas tree towered in the living room and wore glittery ornaments and a spectacular strand of blinking lights. It was topped with a shining silver star. Samantha smiled. For one moment, they were safe.

The Henderson's' enormous large family gathered for the Christmas Eve dinner. At first, Samantha had felt uncomfortable, but everyone made her and the children feel so welcome that she had found herself relaxing for the first time in a long time.

Her eyes caught Harold's, and he smiled back at her. She turned quickly away as she felt Estelle's dagger glare in her direction.

Despite that Samantha had been careful to not show affection for Harold, she could tell Estelle still saw her as a threat. And actually, in a way, Estelle was right to be worried.

After Estelle would leave him in 2001, Samantha and Harold would meet and fall madly in love within the year. They would marry in a lovely ceremony in Niagara Falls and stay happily married forever, oh so Sam hoped.

Despite all the things Sam had felt she lost, God had made up for them all by sending her Harold. Not once, but twice.

Samantha dared glance up at Harold quickly now, and she felt a flush of emotion fill her face. They were still happily married in her mind.

The words on the directions that had accompanied the magical do over cookies came back to her.

"Beware that anything you change in your past may mean that your future changes as well."

Tommy knocked her back to attention as he elbowed her under the table. He made a face at her like this was all too good to be true.

"This food is delicious!" he whispered to his sister, then he took a big chomp on a turkey leg and smiled.

Mrs. Henderson's light eyes glowed at Tommy's open glee and appreciation for the food.

"There's lots of food, sweetheart, help yourself to seconds or thirds."

The group around the table laughed at the child's open exuberance for Mrs. Henderson's cooking.

Tommy smiled back. "I think this is the best thing I've ever eaten!" He turned to his sister, "Don't you think so, Sam?"

Sam ruffled her brother's red curls. "I think it's the best ever!"

It truly was a magnificent feast. They

had fed Trulie earlier, and put the poor exhausted darling to bed.

She was stuffed full of food, warm and safe and tucked in the biggest, softest bed in the lovely guest room Mrs. Henderson had assigned them.

After seconds and some thirds, everyone was stuffed. Mr. Henderson stood and rubbed his stomach. "I suggest we all retire into the living room for some early Christmas presents from Santa."

Tommy's eyes lit up quick with hope and Mr. Henderson winked at him. "Come on, fellow, maybe you can help me pass out the presents. I think I saw something under there with your name on it." Tommy gasped.

Mr. Henderson put his arm around Tommy and said, "Just this way."

"Sure thing!" Tommy said.

Mrs. Henderson gathered the dirty bowls and plates as the rest of the family shuffled into the living room for the next part of the night's festivities.

Samantha hurried to help Mrs. Henderson clear the rest of the plates off the table. Estelle and Harold walked by arm in arm. Estelle clung to him as if he might get away if she unlocked her arm.

As they walked by, Estelle said loudly enough for Sam to hear, "Some people just don't know when they've overstayed their welcome."

Harold's eyes went large and he looked from his fiancée to Samantha, hoping she hadn't heard.

"Hush, Estelle, please. It's Christmas."

She turned and glared at Samantha, openly hostile, and mumbled something

Sam couldn't hear as she pulled Harold into the living room.

Samantha collected the last of the plates and joined Mrs. Henderson in the kitchen where the older woman had started washing dishes. She piled the plates on the counter and started wiping the scraps into the garbage.

Mrs. Henderson turned to her. "Oh, Samantha, how sweet. You don't have to help me, dear; go on in and join in the festivities."

"I want to," Sam said sincerely.

She found a rag and went to the other side of Mrs. Henderson to dry. Mrs. Henderson seemed to look at her as if she remembered her, then turned back to her washing.

"I always dreamed of having a daughter-in-law I could chat with and cook with and, I don't know... just do holiday things..." She smiled at Sam. "I have all boys; it's so nice to have a girl in here with me."

Samantha smiled in understanding. "You have no idea how good it feels to be here too."

She had always loved Mrs. Henderson. And she so yearned to tell her everything. Ask for her help with what to do about Harold…save him somehow from the inevitable pain that she knew lay ahead in the path he was on with Estelle.

But how could she ever explain some zany, back-in-time do over to this dear, traditional woman?

Throughout her time married with Harold, Mrs. Henderson had become like a second mother to Sam. Samantha had felt double blessed by that marriage.

Now being here beside this woman she adored, was oddly both uncomfortable and comforting.

She knew the whole family so well. But they didn't know her.

Sam had already had to catch herself a number of times from asking about one of their jobs or their kids, realizing that that was another time… Her future.
Hopefully.

Sam wondered if she could fix one part of her life, and still keep the people she loved most?

Chapter 36

Macy and her mother laughed across from each other on the floor. Ribbon, wrapping paper, and festive bows littered the floor along with boxes of gifts. Macy smiled as she placed a big silver bow on top of a pretty red package she had wrapped. "This one's for Regina."

Macy had gotten all the children gifts and even a little something for Conner. She had to repay him for cat sitting, after all. She wanted to surprise her mother and he was keeping the little rascal until they could find a way to sneak him in unnoticed.

The doorbell rang and Macy rose. "I'll get it, Mom."

She threw open the door to find Conner standing on the step. Macy's mouth fell open, and she snapped it closed. She peered over his shoulder, looking for the children to come running after him.

He turned and followed her gaze. "You expecting someone?"

Macy cleared her throat. "Um, I thought maybe it was another art day for the kids."

Conner laughed and it went all the way up to his sexy gray eyes. Macy studied her feet.

"Actually, I came by to escort you both to the Silver Bells Christmas Cookie contest this afternoon."

Macy's eyebrow went up.

"I can assure you it's a not-to-be-missed event! Right, Mrs. Kennedy?"

Macy's mom beamed. "Oh, yes, goodness. You must go, Macy; it's the most important event on the mountain all year. Everyone will be there. You know my friends the Landers sisters? Well, go by and say hello for sure; this is their big day."

Macy groaned inwardly at the mention of the Landers, but the Christmas fair was a tempting offer to think about. Not that she had to think long about going on an outing with Conner Anderson, the hunk of Kissing Bridge Mountain.

Macy slid a sideway glance over at him as he ruffled his dark curls free from knit cap.

She sighed and shook her head.

She was really happy that her dream had included a guy interest even if she was about to disappear after Christmas like Cinderella's pumpkin coach.

According to the magical do over cookies, they had one week and it was over at the stroke of midnight on Christmas – just like a fairytale. Kind of. Tomorrow night at twelve it seemed that everything would go poof and this would all be gone.

Macy's heart skipped as a certain fear occurred to her: maybe she wouldn't remember any of this experience after the fact.

Macy went over and hugged her mom tight. Her mother looked up at her in surprise.

"What was that for?"

"Just want you to know how much I really love you, Mom."

Lenora Kennedy's face went through a myriad of emotions. She wiped a tear from her eye and smiled. As she went to get up from the floor, Macy saw her reach out one hand and grab the side of the sofa for balance.

"Are you sure you're all right, Mom?"

She smiled weakly. "I'm fine, just old." She laughed. "You two go along and enjoy yourselves; the Christmas fair is one of the best events all year."

Conner nodded. "Pretty much the biggest event all year. So what do you say, Macy, you want to go?"

Macy looked back and forth between them, unsure.

Her mother waved them along. "Go! Have fun, dears. I've got loads of things to make for the Christmas dinner at the Landers' house tomorrow. I promised Carol I'd make my garlic cauliflower soufflé and a veggie plate. I'll get started on that. You two young people go have fun."

Macy rolled her eyes at the mention of the Landers house for Christmas dinner.

Her mother continued. "Of course you're invited too, Conner."

Conner beamed. "Well, thank you Mrs. Kennedy. I'm sure it will be quite a festive occasion after winning the blue ribbon again."

Macy tilted her head. "How do you know that they're already going to win the blue ribbon? I thought the cookie contest whatever it's called – was just starting?"

"Silver Bells Christmas Cookie Contest," Conner and Macy's mom said at once.

Macy took a breath; this really was Christmas-land here in Kissing Bridge.

"Okay, yeah, how do you know those Landers ladies are going to win already?"

Macy's mom waved her hand. "Oh, Landers ladies have been winning the contest for over fifty years now. The town rumor is that their mother Izzy has an enchanted recipe book hidden away somewhere, and that's how they've managed to keep a lock on that blue ribbon! Isn't that right, Conner?"

Conner nodded. "Yep. Ms. Carol and Ms. Ethel are the reigning cookie queens of Kissing Bridge, undeniably. They do make some magical cookies."

Macy gasped.

"Did you say magical?"

Conner laughed.

"Don't take everything so literal, Ms. Lawyer-to-Be."

Macy laughed back at him. "I'd love to go, but I kind of had some other plans."

Macy was not about to leave her mother unattended after the episode she had witnessed earlier. If her mother wasn't up to coming with them, then she was going to make Christmas Eve special right there at home.

She cocked her head to one side conspiratorially and winked at Conner. "It's Christmas Eve and I think it's the perfect time to watch a mushy movie! I mean, *Miracle on 34th Street* must be on; they play it every year, you can barely get away from it!"

Conner and her mother looked up at her oddly.

"I mean, wouldn't this be the perfect time to stay in and decorate?" Macy said.

Mrs. Kennedy looked back and forth between the two young people.

Conner nodded his head and smiled broadly at Macy in understanding.

"Yes, I do believe you're right, and I think I may have just what we need in the truck."

Macy donned her mom's big ugly parka and her new snow boots to follow him out.

"Come on, I'll help you unload it," she whispered.

Soon they were back in the warm house with bags and bags of decorations and ornaments. Mrs. Kennedy came out from the kitchen with some hot apple cider and put it down on the table. She looked at the bounty and brought a delicate hand to her mouth.

Next Conner came dragging a beautiful Christmas tree behind him. Macy pointed to the corner across from the sofa, and he erected it easily and tightened the stand so it stood tall and strong.

They all looked up at it. It was glorious and reached clear to the top of the tall ceiling. Macy's mom put her hand over her heart and her sweet brown eyes glistened with tears of joy which brimmed at the edges as each new delight was unveiled.

"Surprise, Mom!" Macy said delightedly. "I thought we needed a bit more Christmas spirit in the house! I hope that's alright with you?"

"Oh, darling! I'm thrilled, just thrilled." She leafed through the boxes of ornaments and shook her head. "You bought the children's homemade ornaments?"

Macy nodded. "They were the best! Who wants those fancy-schmancy ones from China when I can get the best craftsmen from Kissing Bridge?"

Conner unloaded two matching snowmen lamps and placed them on the end tables by the sofa. Macy ran over excitedly and plugged them in, and the snowmen's heads lit up bright and glowed. Her mom's eyebrows lifted at the sight of them.

"And how did I ever get by without these fabulous snowmen lanterns?" Mrs.

Kennedy chuckled as she ran her hand over one corncob nose.

Macy hugged her mother again with force. "I love you, Mom."

Mrs. Kennedy looked up at her daughter with warmth.

"You're looking at me like you're never going to see me again darling, when this is just the beginning. A great, new, beautiful beginning!"

Lenora glowed with joy. How many years she had dreamed of this, and now here they were together.

Suddenly, she gasped in horror as a huge Santa head bobbed in front of the picture window. "What...?!"

Macy ran to the window and looked outside and laughed. "And I hope you love the huge blow-up Santa that's going in your front yard!"

They both watched as Conner wrestled with the massive balloon figure outside.

The big Santa seemed to be getting the better of him.

Macy went to the door. "I better see if he needs some help."

The cold outdoor air brought a blush to Macy's cheeks. Conner was pumping up Santa with something that resembled a bicycle pump.

She went and stood next to him as he huffed and puffed with the cumbersome blow-up decoration.

"Need some help?" Macy joked.

Conner conceded. "Yes, if you could just get ahold of his boots while I pump, I think we can get the air in better."

After fifteen minutes, the sun had slipped behind the mountains, but they had succeeded. The massive blow-up Santa now stood proudly with one balloon mitten hand raised in holiday welcome.

"Good job!" Macy said. "It looks beautiful!"

Conner looked at her. "You look beautiful."

Macy swallowed and blushed.

"That thing," Conner motioned toward the huge Santa bobbing happily in the wind, "looks Christmas appropriate."

They both laughed.

Conner tucked his hands in his pockets.

"Well, it's Christmas Eve and…."

Macy cut in. "I understand. I'm sure you want to get to the fair and see all your friends." She smiled warmly. "It's nice to live in a place where people know you, and care." She trailed off. "I don't want to keep you."

Conner nodded. "I appreciate that."

Macy's heart sank.

She only had until tomorrow, and already she wanted to spend more time with this man. She turned away from his gaze so he wouldn't see the play of emotions on her face.

Conner cut into her thoughts. "But I'm pretty sure you're going to need some help getting that star on the top of the tree. I think you might need a big tall man to come to your aid. Star hanging is very complicated you know."

Macy looked at Conner. "You offering?"

Conner hummed playfully and Macy caught sight of a dimple. "Thought you'd never ask. I'd love to spend Christmas Eve with you, Macy."

She looked up into his gorgeous gray eyes sparkling in the moonlight that had just made its appearance. The yard was alight with the big full moon, and the attraction between them was undeniable.

Macy had to stop herself from throwing herself into his arms. All she needed was to fall in love with a man that was going to be gone. Another doomed relationship.

Macy's heart caught.

Only where before she could mentally write off most of her other beaus as wrong for her, there was *nothing she wouldn't miss about Conner.*

She bit her lip and looked up at the man she had come to care for so much. This time she had gotten herself in deeper than she had planned.

"I'm so happy." The truth fell out of her mouth.

Conner wrapped an arm around her and pointed up at the sky. "Look, it's the blue moon. They say it's very unusual for a blue moon at Christmas. It's kind of magical, don't you think? Maybe it's a sign from the heavens?"

Macy's body shivered at the mention of magic. Hers was about to end, and more than anything she wished it would go on forever.

She turned to the handsome man that she had grown to care about despite all her attempts to stop herself.

"Conner, I have to tell you something. Full disclosure. This may be a dream."

Conner peered down at her with a mirthful smile.

"I completely agree!" He said. "And one I never intend to wake up from."

Macy caught her breath and sucked back her feelings. Could Conner possibly be feeling the same way she was? Because right now, all she wanted was to throw herself into those big muscled arms.

As if reading her desire, Conner wrapped his arms around her and pulled her close. He kissed her tenderly, and Macy melted into him as if she and he were one.

Chapter 37

Mrs. Henderson reached out unexpectedly and put an arm around Sam. "I'm really happy you're here, Samantha, and your brother and sister. Merry Christmas."

Samantha looked back at her. "Merry Christmas, Mrs. Henderson."

Estelle flung open the kitchen door just then, startling them both. Samantha dropped a teacup and it broke on the floor tile. Samantha gasped and fumbled to pick up the pieces. "Oh, I'm so sorry. It just slipped out of my hands…"

Mrs. Henderson looked at Estelle with little love in her eyes.

"What is it, Estelle?"

She turned up her nose. "You better come see right away."

Samantha continued retrieving the pieces of the cup and apologizing.

"I'm so sorry; I'll pay you for it..."

"Don't worry about it, Samantha. It's just an old cup. No harm done."

Mrs. Henderson patted her back as she followed Estelle out the room.

Samantha scooped up the last bits and put them in the garbage. An eerie tingling ran inside her. She went out to the dining room to see if they had cleared the whole table, and if she could do anything else to help out.

The TV played in the dining room and Estelle and Mrs. Henderson were glued to it.

As if in slow motion, Sam could see the rest of the happy group assembled around the Christmas tree. Tommy was reading names and handing out gifts proudly, as if he had bought them himself.

An urgent sounding reporter on the TV spoke with an important breaking news update. Samantha froze when she heard her name come from the TV. The reporter was showing a close up shot of an old family picture. Samantha's family.

Sam gasped.

The reporter continued to announce an amber alert for all three of the Myers children, and an emergency number to call for anyone who had any news about them to contact the police immediately.

Mrs. Henderson and Estelle both turned as one to stare at Samantha.

Estelle had a sick little smile of satisfaction on her face.

"I knew they weren't friends of the family. I've no idea why Harold lied or why he stopped to pick up this group of vagabonds." She spat out the words like venom. Her hatred palatable.

Mrs. Henderson turned to Estelle. "You shush! This is none of your concern, Estelle." She turned and caught sight of Samantha's face now pure white.

Mrs. Henderson took Samantha's hand and looked at Estelle with meaning. "It's Christmas Eve and these people are our guests. Tonight we're going to focus on Christmas."

Sam was stuck like glue to the carpet with Merry Christmas tunes drifting around her in a haze.

"Is that okay with you, Samantha?" Samantha nodded from outside herself. She felt as if she were floating.

Estelle opened her mouth to argue, and Mrs. Henderson said again more firmly,

"I hope I made it more than clear, Estelle, that I don't want what we just learned here going out of this room. Do you understand?"

Estelle nodded reluctantly, but Samantha caught the mischievous curl on the right side of her mouth.

Sam's heart sank.

Now Estelle had all the ammo she needed to make Samantha disappear.

Worse than humiliating her in front of all the Henderson clan, or Harold, the thought that this woman was truly capable of calling the police and turning them into her father at any moment was chilling.

Her father would never forgive her; who knew what he would do this time to her, and poor Tommy.

She didn't trust Estelle, and Sam knew she was darn right not to.

Chapter 38

Everyone gathered around the Christmas tree to open gifts. Even Trulie woke for the grand festivity. They had never had a family celebration like this and Sam didn't want Trulie missing it.

Samantha sat with a big smile and a sinking heart as she watched Trulie tottering around, playing with the wrapping paper as if it were the best gift in the world.

When Tommy handed her a present, the little girl didn't even know what to do with it. She turned to the group of onlookers who applauded her curiously.

Tommy crouched and helped his little sister open the surprise. Inside was a brand new doll that looked a lot like Trulie herself. The tot's eyes went so round she looked like a cartoon character. She looked around the group again, unsure.

"It's a doll, Trulie," Tommy said reassuringly. "It's really for you." He unpacked the beautiful doll and put it in her hands. She hugged it and wrapped her pink blanket around it as if to make sure it would be warm.

Sam brought her hand to her heart at the touching scene. She smiled at Mrs. Henderson for her kindness and mouthed a silent, "Thank you." Mrs. Henderson winked back at her.

Somehow, the sweet lady had managed to rummage up some gifts that were appropriate for her brother and sister, and Samantha didn't think she'd seen them looking so happy ever.

Tommy actually had three presents with his name on them, and it wasn't even Christmas yet. He relinquished his present passing job to play with the huge Star Wars LEGO set Santa had brought him, and now Mr. Henderson was on the carpet next to him, helping put it together and discussing the pros and cons of where to place each piece.

Harold took over the job of gift giver and rustled through the remaining presents and passed them out.

Mr. Henderson got a new pipe that he seemed to adore, and Mrs. Henderson was not so happy about it from the look on her face.

John Henderson, Harold's oldest brother, got a pair of skis and everyone *oohed* and *ahhed*. He kissed his pretty wife, Janice. "Just what I wanted!"

Janice laughed. "Good thing, because I'm pretty sure you guessed what they were even with my creative wrapping!"
Everyone laughed.

Harold came over with a lovely silver package topped with a sprig of holly and a little card with Samantha's name on it.

"This one's for you, Samantha," he said with a smile as he held it out to her.

Estelle looked over from her huge pile of gifts and gave Samantha a nasty look.

Samantha looked away. "A gift for me?"

She unwrapped the paper and unveiled a light turquoise homemade knitted scarf and hat. "Oh my goodness, this is beautiful." She pulled it out of the box and showed it to the family.

Mrs. Henderson beamed at her from her place on the couch. "Try it on, darling, try it on!"

Sam wrapped it around her neck and snuggled into it. Mrs. Henderson clapped with joy. "I think it matches your eyes perfectly– don't you think, Harold?"

Harold looked at the scarf highlighting Sam's already bright green eyes. The turquoise material added an extra blue tinge that made them sparkle even brighter. Harold was lost in them.

He mumbled in answer, "Yes I do."

Chapter 39

Naomi's nurse, Purnell, came in with a small decorated Christmas tree. "Surprise!" She clapped her hands. "Purnell! How nice!"

Purnell plugged it in and tiny lights blinked on. "You're welcome. Too much stimulus isn't great when you're in the first couple days of recovery, but it's Christmas tomorrow. Feels like the room could use some holiday help."

Naomi giggled in agreement. "Between the hundred degree California weather and the white walls, I almost forgot it was Christmas."

The rehab was in Palm Springs, and outside was a searing hot desert without even a tinseled cactus to brighten things up.

Purnell adjusted Naomi's tubes. She hated to see herself looking so weak and helpless.

"You must get tired of dealing with all these losers that come in here after wrecking their lives, and you have to pick up the pieces." Naomi said.

The nurse looked at her, then he shook his head.

"Losers? I think of you as a survivor."

Naomi's words stuck in her throat.

Purnell fluffed her pillow.

"You're going to be okay, Naomi. You have a goal. That's what you told me, right?"

Naomi nodded.

"I want to win the Gold at the Olympics." Somehow she found the confidence to raise her voice louder. "I want to be a symbol of what you can do, for the other kids. So it's bigger than me. I need to represent."

From her bed, she threw up her arms outstretched as if she were crossing the finish line as a winner, nearly pulling out the cord to the machine.

Purnell pointed at her. "After you're out of here please!" He moved over and readjusted the cord and checked her arm. He shook his head.

"See, now that is passion! You're a winner! You're going to do just fine when you get out of here. Gonna make us proud."

Naomi felt warmer with him near.

Purnell moved to the door, but he had to look back. "Just remember, Naomi King. Addiction isn't your future. You just got off track."

Naomi cocked her head and they laughed at his unintended pun.

"We all have high hopes for you." He winked and pulled the door closed.

Chapter 40

It was Christmas Eve and the bulk of the rehab and clinic staff had left.

Purnell was the only nurse on staff, and he was stuck with nothing to do but check in on Naomi, who was the only one left in the clinic. Her official last day of detox was today, so she would be able to join the main group in the rehab for the Christmas festivities tomorrow and the holiday sober party they had put together.

Purnell had surprised her and snuck in both a TV and a doggie bag from the main house's lunch which was made by their five-star chef for the Christmas Eve lunch.

Naomi was just getting her strength back and had been barely able to eat anything. But this smelled way better than the clinic's mashed potatoes and Jell-O dishes.

"Is this vegan again?" said Naomi. It may have smelled good, but it looked too healthy to be true.

Purnell chuckled and glanced at the Hallmark Christmas marathon she was watching. "Come on, Naomi, at least try the darn vegan turkey dinner! It's almost as good as the real thing."

She shook her head. "Isn't bad enough they make us be sober without forcing this horrible, healthy vegan food on us? How about some pizza? Grease and pepperoni? Now shhhh! They have Santa on trial and they're just about to bring in all the mail. This is my favorite part."

Purnell stood in front of the TV.

"Ha! Now I have AMMO!"

Naomi tried to look around him. But Purnell stayed put with his hands on his hips. He looked like Superman in scrubs.

Naomi laughed.

"Don't make me get out of this hospital bed, Purnell!"

But Purnell just shrugged. "Okay, you win. Don't eat. I just don't know how you are supposed to be an Olympic winner if you don't keep your strength up and feed your beautiful self. Darn shame."

Naomi looked up at him. "Are you flirting with me or you just trying to keep me alive?"

Chapter 41

It was Christmas morning in the Henderson home. The chords of Bing Cosby's "White Christmas" filled the house and Samantha's heart. Smells of baking bread and sweet apple cider wafted up the stairs from the kitchen below.

Samantha rummaged through her satchel for something appropriate to wear at a rich person's house for a holiday breakfast. She had only packed a few outfits. Not that she had a huge wardrobe. Most of it was bought from the secondhand store. Still, she had a found a few nice pieces of clothes on discount that were classy and well made. Her Anne Klein knit red sweater and pencil dark jeans would be perfect. She hoped.

She steadied her breathing as she brushed her hands through her long blonde hair and washed her face. She looked at her big green eyes and her hand strayed instinctively to the side of her jaw that she was so used to seeing sunken, broken, and deformed.

She usually took great care to cover her scar because the deep purple was hard to camouflage. Now her face was clear and unblemished. How different her life might have been if this were reality.

She sighed. She had to figure out a plan to save the kids, no matter what happened. The future as she knew it was horrible and sad. Tommy would end up hanging himself, his will to live broken and abused.

And poor, innocent sweet Trulie would run away from home, never to be heard from again.

Samantha went over and kissed Trulie on the face and smiled. *Things will be different this time, Trulie,* she swore to her silently. *For all of us.*

Sam walked down the hall and peeked in the door to the adjoining room to check on Tommy. He slept like a baby. His usually tough face looked peaceful and serene. Sam's throat caught at the sweet sight; suddenly he looked like the eight-year-old he was instead of the sixteen-year-old he pretended to be. Samantha brought her hand to her heart.

But what about Harold? Her heart sunk at the thought of a life without him. She had no idea how their romance would turn out, or if they'd ever even meet again after this.

She heard Harold's voice down the hall and froze. She loved Harold from the bottom of her toes to the top of her head. In the future reality, it broke his heart just as much as it broke hers that they hadn't been able to have a family.

Samantha wondered if this could be destiny's way of saving Harold?

Despite their deep love, maybe Harold would've been better without her. Maybe Estelle would soften with motherhood and they would have their own children and in the end his life would turn out great.

Samantha wiped away a tear and shuffled down the rosewood staircase.

The only people awake were Mrs. Henderson and Harold.

Sam looked around, confused. "I heard the music; I thought everyone was up."

Harold winked at Samantha. "We're the early birds, I guess."

Bacon sizzled in two skillets and unbroken eggs filled a wooden bowl. Mrs. Henderson looked at the contents and shook her head.

"This is not going to be enough food for our hoard! Harold, why don't you take Samantha outside and show her the chicken coop?"

Samantha's eyebrows rose.

Harold huffed. "What's she saying, Sam, is why don't you and I freeze our butts off

walking out to the chicken coop to get
more eggs."

Samantha laughed. "I'm in!"

Harold smiled back.

Samantha looked up at Harold as they
walked through the snow-filled country
yard. How many times had they trekked
this path together? She had seen his
parents' glorious yard in every season.
Harold and she loved to walk the farm,
holding hands and planning their
retirement; living off-grid and growing
their own food; canning it for the winter.
Simple and easy, peaceful and joyful – just
like now.

Harold suddenly turned as if reading her thoughts. Or remembering.

"Gosh, Samantha, I...I feel like I've known you for a long time. It's a weird feeling."

Sam wanted to tell him everything, if only she could.

"We always felt that way."

He glanced oddly at her use of past tense.

"I mean, I felt like it's just easy to be around you," she amended. Harold looked at her for a long time and Samantha didn't turn away.

"Did you ever hang out over in Enchanted Oaks...?" he questioned. "Shopping or going to any of the restaurants?"

Samantha shook her head. "No. I pretty much just take care of my brother and sister and, well, I'm an actress."

"An actress?"

"Yes, I love it actually. I minored in theatre. Not that I get to do it a lot, but I just played Juliet."

Harold blinked and lowered his head in awe. "Shakespeare no less?'

Sam didn't answer, but blushed.

"Wow," said Harold. "I can see you would make a fabulous Juliet; I bet you're very talented."

Samantha grinned. He was so – Harold! Supporting and encouraging and yet he barely knew her.

She chided him. "You're just being nice. Besides, as much as I like to think I could just move to Hollywood and become a movie star...what are the chances?"

"Good!" Harold said sincerely.

Sam sputtered "You don't even know me! How can you believe in me? My father said I should be taking typing classes so I can get a good secretary job."

Harold stopped in his tracks and looked at her sincerely. "Because you have an authenticity; a truth, and to tell you honestly Samantha, it's downright refreshing and unique. The movies would be lucky to cast you."

Samantha had to stop from throwing herself into his arms right then. Instead she joked.

"Maybe you need to be my agent."

Harold scratched his chin. "I think I'd like that."

They laughed together as Harold opened the chicken coop and showed her how he collected the eggs.

"First, I talk low and sweet, and then I just reach in and grab them."

He commenced to do just that. Soon he had a dozen, and they trudged back through the falling snow with the warm eggs wrapped in a basket.

"Where were you going when I picked you up? You don't have to tell me if you don't want to, but I won't think of you any differently and I won't judge you. I just want to help for some reason."

Samantha looked at the man she loved so much. Was he always her destiny? He looked so young and happy. Without a care in the world. Right now Harold was just a handsome guy with his whole life ahead of him and hope in his heart. Raised by a healthy family, he never even saw the way life was about to side slam him.

In real life they had met in group therapy in New York City. Harold had been getting over the betrayal and loss of not only his wife, Estelle, but her confession that the baby girl he raised as his own the last five years was also gone and had never been biologically his anyway. The dreams Harold had given up to provide for them by working mundane jobs that crushed his soul were immeasurable.

Should Samantha tell Harold the truth about Estelle right now? Wouldn't it be the right thing to do to warn him and save him from this pain? Were the magical Christmas do over cookies actually meant for him?

Pain filled Samantha's eyes and tears sprung up suddenly, causing her to reach out for balance.

She had come back in time and been given a second chance to make things right, but she wasn't sure how to do it.

Harold reached out to support her. "Samantha? Are you okay?"

She fought back the emotion flooding her.

"I just need to throw some water on my face; I have a bit of a headache." She wiped her eyes fiercely and hurried toward the kitchen ahead of Harold.

"Samantha!" He called after her, but she ran through the snow with the tears blinding her eyes.

Chapter 42

Samantha bent over the kitchen sink, throwing water on her face, when she noticed she was not alone. She turned, and Harold's mother was looking at her questioningly, with a glint of sorrow in her dark blue eyes.

She moved to the refrigerator, opened it silently, and removed a carton of eggnog. She took two glasses from the cupboard and filled them both, then put them on the table.

"Come sit with me." Her voice was gentle, as if Samantha were a deer that might run from the headlights of her presence. "I want to talk about what's going on with your father."

Samantha cast her eyes away in shame.

Mrs. Henderson reached out and touched Sam's arm lightly, as if not to scare her.

"I can see the bruises on Tommy and I noticed you walking with stiffness that didn't seem normal for a spritely seventeen-year-old."

Sam glanced up from beneath her lashes and her cheeks flamed red as she met Mrs. Henderson's kind gaze.

"I suspect you have a reason to be hiding from your father. Am I right?"

Samantha swallowed guiltily and nodded.

Harold's mother continued in a soft, reassuring tone. "I want to help you, Samantha."

"My father... he's powerful Mrs.

Henderson. Thank you so much, but you want to stay clear of us. He's a policeman; they all stick together in this town. I don't want to put your family in danger."

Mrs. Henderson's eyes filled with anger and her mouth became a tight line. She got up and walked around the room. And then looked back at Samantha with a newfound defiant stance and put her hands on her hips.

"Well we're not powerful. We're just a normal family, but my brother is a judge and his wife works for social services and a judge pulls way more weight than a cop. Especially after he gets an earful from me!"

Hope filled Samantha's large green eyes, but she had already seen how things could go wrong just when she thought they were going right. She had saved the money, she had brought the kids, and still things had not gone as planned.

Mrs. Henderson noticed her silence and brushed a soft hand on Sam's cheek. "You're quite grown up and mature for a girl your age. You've been a brave sister. But you deserve a chance too, darling."

Samantha sniffed back a tear and her heart caught at the woman's kindness. Mrs. Henderson smiled at her.

"You think about it, okay? If you want me to step in, you only need to say so. Whatever you decide, I'll back you."

Sam gave a huge sigh. "I don't want to seem ungrateful. You're the kindest woman I've ever met. But I am in charge of my brother and sister. I'm the one that has to make sure everything turns out right for them."

She looked up at the older woman.

"You understand, right?"

Mrs. Henderson nodded. "More than you know, darling. Family is the most important thing in the world and I admire you, Samantha. But what is your plan exactly, if you don't mind my asking?"

"Well… "Sam stammered to answer her question, and the truth came out. "I don't have a plan Mrs. Henderson. I had some money and a plan but both of them are gone now.

Chapter 43

Carol Landers welcomed everybody at her door with a hug and a hearty "Merry Christmas!" The nerves in Macy's stomach tightened as she stamped her feet on the welcome mat. Carol ushered them in to join the party of friends and family that had gathered around the big table at Carol's house.

Everyone echoed choruses of hellos and Merry Christmas.

The kitchen was in an uproar of cooking frenzy as Macy and her mom brought their food in for instructions from Ethel. Carol's energetic younger sister was a spritely AARP member that was serious about her baking. Right now she was barking out orders in the back like Patton to his troops.

"Summer, stir the gravy constantly–no breaks or it will get lumps.

Brad, honey, you slice the turkey at an angle."

Her eagle eyes suddenly lit on Macy and her mom standing by the kitchen door with their baked dishes.

Ethel wiped her hands on her apron and came to greet them. She was all smiles.

"Lenora, Macy, Merry Christmas! Thank you for bringing the dip; you know it's our favorite." She kissed Macy's mom on the cheek and lifted the side of tinfoil from her bowl. "Mmm, that looks wonderful! Mashed potatoes with bacon and cheese; and my favorite cauliflower dip it must be Christmas!" They all laughed.

"The boys will love it! Just put them down on the table, girls."

Carol Landers pulled out an old fashioned triangle and rang it. "Time for Christmas dinner, everyone!"

The Christmas feast was laid before them in all its splendor. There were friends and neighbors and family: too many to remember.

Her mom tried to help in whispers. "That beautiful young lady is Ethel's daughter, and that's her boyfriend, Brad Anderson–he's Conner's brother." Macy looked over and smiled at the couple.

"That's Earl; he runs the Eagle's Peak Lodge. And over there is Mr. Johnston and his wife, Bertha, and Dolly...." Macy's eyebrows rose as she studied Dolly in her complete elf outfit. From her toes to her long, pointed, bell-adorned hat, she made the perfect Santa's helper.

Macy ogled at the odd characters that made up this crazy Christmas-loving town. She would miss it.

Macy reached over the table and grabbed her mother's hand. This was the happiest Christmas she had ever had, and maybe would ever have, and if it was a dream, Macy didn't want to wake up from it. But as she glanced up at Aunt Carol, she saw something in her eyes, and she knew. This moment wouldn't last forever, and this all was a dream.

All Macy had was right now, and right now was that miracle.

Suddenly she was startled by a deep voice behind her. "Is this seat taken, miss?"

Macy's heart caught in her throat as Conner pulled out the chair next to her.

"Merry Christmas, everyone." He greeted the group. "Sorry I was late."

Carol waved away his worries. "Anytime is perfect. Happy to have you!"

Conner sat down next to Macy and her entire body tingled.

He leaned over intimately and whispered, "Merry Christmas, Macy."

She looked into his gray eyes and felt as if time stood still.

Carol cleared her throat and stood, tinging her glass with her fork. "Before we have our Christmas feast, which I hope you all love because we've been cooking all morning–"

Ethel came in with a basket of hot rolls just then and put them in the center of the table with finality and interjected. "So if you don't like the food, how about making my Christmas and *not* mentioning it?"

The crowd laughed and then clapped for the masterpiece of culinary perfection spread before them.

Ethel took her seat and got comfortable. "Sorry, sis, go ahead."

Carol raised an arm at Ethel. "Well done, Ethel. Everything looks incredible." She turned serious for a moment and looked around at the table of loved ones seated before her.

"I'd like to take a moment to personally welcome Macy to our table this Christmas. It's a truly magical day." Everyone nodded and clapped in agreement.

Carol continued. "In honor of your being here, Macy, perhaps you'd like to say the prayer before we eat?"

Macy sunk into herself and looked awkwardly around the table. Was this the time to mention she was an atheist? Not a great subject to bring up on Christmas with all these Christmas-loving people. She had no idea how to say a prayer or where to even start.

Conner saw her confusion and fear and leaned over and said in a whisper,

"Just speak from your heart."

Speak from her heart.

"Well…" She wobbled a little as she stood. "I want to thank the Landers, without which none of this would be possible…" She looked at Carol and she winked at her.

Macy continued. "For inviting me here tonight, for the feast they've made, and for all of you."

Macy's throat swelled up and she stopped, unsure of what to say. Conner reached over and took her hand and squeezed it tight. Macy swallowed and found her voice.

"And even though I'm not personally acquainted with God, I feel that it's only appropriate that I thank God at this moment for all of you, for all of this, and mostly for my mother." She looked down at the woman she had come to love so very much. "I love you, Mom." Tears welled up in her eyes now and she said quickly, "Amen."

"Amen," came the chorus around the table. And the celebration of Christmas began.

Chapter 44

Naomi was in the middle of a Hallmark Christmas marathon when she heard the light tapping at her door. She ran her hands through her hair and sat up in bed, excited to see Purnell. It was Christmas, and he had promised he would sit through the entire mushy marathon in return for her eating whatever he brought.

Unfortunately, he had ruled out the coconut pie and chocolate cake she had requested as being too unhealthy, but he hadn't said no to the pizza, so she had high hopes.

The door opened, and Naomi turned in anticipation of seeing Purnell's bounty.

She caught her breath and her heart skipped instead. It wasn't Purnell. It was Leroy.

Naomi gasped. "Leroy! What...what are you doing here? You can't be here! If they catch you, you're going to get in trouble."

Leroy laughed as he shut the door behind him and locked it, then came over and sat down roughly on her bed.

"What you talking about, baby? Do you think I'm worried about the guards at the rehab or what the nurse says?" He looked around the room. "Where's your shit? Let's go."

Naomi looked at him, confused. "Go? I'm detoxing, Leroy. I'm trying to get better."

He came over and kissed her hard on the lips. He tasted of sweat and beer. She pulled back, repulsed.

"What, no love for Leroy now you've been in some fancy center for rich drug addicts? Don't forget where you came from. You ain't no better and you never will be."

Fear ran through Naomi like a chilly gust of wind. The Hallmark movie ran in the background in direct contrast to her reality at this moment.

She pointed at the tube in her arm and the machine and tried to talk sense into Leroy. He was usually drunk, but he seemed extra hyped up tonight and she wondered what he was intoxicated with.

"You look fine to me." He yanked the needle out of her arm and the machine complained with a loud beeping alarm. Leroy looked at Naomi triumphantly. "That was easy. Come on, move your ass before some idiot comes to find out why this machine is going off."

He spotted the plug and went over and tugged the cord out of the wall. The alarm stopped.

Naomi pulled herself up to the side of the bed and rubbed her arm where the needle had been yanked out. "Leroy, what are you doing here and how did you even find me?"

"Save the questions, baby. I've got my buddy Roger outside and he's charging me by the hour. Besides, we just scored some new pills for you you'll love."

Naomi started to panic. He knew how to hit her weak spot.

"Leroy, I don't want to go."

He pulled out a handful of capsules. "Nirvana, baby. It's all right here waiting for you. They brainwashed you in this place."

Naomi's eyes widened, and she reached instinctively for the bag.

Suddenly there was a knock at the door, and Purnell was calling her name.

"Naomi? Are you all right?"

Leroy put his finger to his mouth and his other hand over Naomi's mouth from behind.

Purnell fumbled with the door handle, then unlocked it with his universal key. He stepped into the room and froze. He took in the situation and the nasty look on Leroy's face.

"How did you get in here?"

Leroy gave him a churly look, "What's up with you guys in blue scrubs? What are you, a girly man nurse? I'm talking to my lady. Get out of here; it's none of your business."

Purnell looked distressed, and Naomi just wanted to tell him the truth. She didn't want anything to do with Leroy; she wanted to get healthy and she wanted to earn the respect that Purnell had given her. She wanted to be the best she could be for herself and for every little kid in the neighborhood that had ever looked up to her, and counted on her to be something. Not a loser, not a victim of the neighborhood, not a victim of color.

Purnell cast his eyes away from Leroy and focused on Naomi, "Are you okay?"

Naomi was shaken to the core, and her yearning for the drug was more than she could handle. She looked at Leroy and what he had in his hand. She didn't know what to do, but she knew Leroy was dangerous. If she could just get him out of the rehab maybe she could talk sense into him and get him to leave quietly.

Naomi stood up tall in her hospital gown. She turned to Purnell and looked him in the eye. "I'm gonna leave, Purnell."

With that, she turned to her loser boyfriend. "Leroy, help me get my things."

Purnell tried to stop her.

"No, please, Naomi! Don't do this! You're not well yet, you can't."

Naomi put her hand on his arm lightly. "Look, Purnell, being sober just isn't for me. Just let me go." The lie fell off her lips so easily.

She watched Leroy nervously as he twisted his gold rings on his fingers; they were better than steel knuckles, and how he really hurt people on the street that didn't pay up.

Purnell wasn't giving up on her.

"Naomi, this is the old you talking; these are the old, unhealthy patterns talking, the part of you that doesn't love yourself, the part of you that doesn't think you're worth something! Naomi, you are worth something! You are amazing!"

Naomi had her head down, gathering her things and hiding the tears welling up in her eyes when suddenly she heard a terrible pound and crunch as Leroy's punch hit hard.

Purnell keeled over backwards and his head hit the side of the desk. He fell on the floor with a sickening thud. Naomi watched in horror as blood trickled from his head. She screamed and ran to him. He was alive but unconscious.

"What did you do?" Naomi shrieked at Leroy. She pushed past him and ran out of the room and down the hall of the clinic, screaming for help. "Help! Please, someone! Help!"

They'd taken away her cell phone and most of the staff were gone for the holidays. The place was empty. She ran down the hall in her hospital gown looking for an emergency phone, and looking over her shoulder in case Leroy came after her.

She heard the sounds of Christmas music and people, and turned toward them. The main door to the rehab must be that way.

She ran down the hall and flung open a door.

It was the nurse's office, empty now, with what looked to be connecting doors that led to the main rehab center.

Naomi picked up the phone on the nurse's desk and fiddled with it trying to get an outside line. Suddenly, she heard footsteps hurriedly approaching and Leroy yelling her name.

Naomi threw the phone down and raced for the door. She threw it open and ran down the hall toward the main room as fast as she could. She could nearly feel Leroy's breath on her cheek, when she burst into the midst of the rehab center and a fancy, dressy Christmas party. Leroy quickly ducked back into the shadows.

The party stopped at her sudden entrance and the sight of Naomi in her hospital gown and absolute dismay.

"Call a doctor; Purnell's been hurt!" She screamed, "And call the cops there's a crazy man back there."

All Naomi remembered was the sea of concerned faces staring at her, and Leroy's back as he ran away, before she fainted and everything went black.

Chapter 45

The kids played with their new toys under the massive Christmas tree, giggling and making pretend sound effects. Sam felt a sense of peace she had never experienced. How many times she had wished she could have brought her sister and brother over to a place like this.

As they played, Samantha went upstairs to tidy up their rooms. She pulled up the comforter to make the bed when she heard arguing.

She made herself smaller and sunk back down the hallway so as not to intrude. It was Harold and Estelle.

But Samantha kept hearing her name. She was three steps down the stairs when Estelle burst open the door and came storming two steps at a time at Sam.

She knocked into Sam with a force, and Samantha grabbed the railing. For a moment she felt as if fate was about to rise up and snag her despite all her efforts.

Estelle was breathing fire and her hot breath lifted Sam's hair.

"I don't know what you think you're doing, getting involved with my fiancé, but I'm pregnant, missy, and he is going to marry me, so just stay away from him!"

Estelle's teeth were gritted. Samantha opened her mouth. She wanted to say so much to this horrible person that would hurt her husband so badly. Instead she simply said, "Really? Has Harold had a DNA test to see if that baby is really his, Estelle?"

Estelle reacted as if she'd been hit in the face. She pulled back and lifted a threatening finger.

"You don't know anything you piece of trash, and don't think I won't call your father if you even make a peep about a DNA test."

Before Samantha could agree, Estelle pushed her as hard as she could with both hands. Samantha felt her feet leave the ground as she nosedived down the long, hard staircase.

Chapter 46

The large rehab, though dripping in the latest holiday garb, felt hollow and empty and sad as if the walls somehow echoed the pain over what had occurred to Purnell.

The rehab attendant had called an emergency group therapy session for the people that were still there, and Naomi had been moved into her own room and out of the detox clinic.

Naomi was out of her mind with grief. Shame and guilt flooded her as she realized that she had almost ruined her life all over again. Almost betrayed Coach West again.

Worst of all partly to blame for hurting this wonderful man, Purnell, that had done nothing but try to help her.

This was supposed to be her second chance. Her do-over. Was she just destined to have a horrible, useless life where good people would be better off away from her?

Amidst the hushed voices in the group therapy room, Naomi picked out bits of people sharing their feelings about what had happened to Purnell and the depth of where addiction could bring you.

Somewhere in the middle of the meeting, Naomi stumbled out of the room and found herself barefoot and outside, staring up at the cloudless Christmas day sky.

It was a brisk day for Californian standards, but she ambled down the small stone path that led to the chapel on the outskirts of the property.

The doors were open, and she could see the sun streaming through the stained glass windows.

Naomi had never felt the need to pray more. She fell to her knees and clasped her hands together. "Please, God," she prayed, "give me the strength to get through this, and give Purnell the strength to get through this too.

My life might not be worth much, but I swear to you, God, I swear, that if Purnell is okay, I will never do drugs again. I will believe in miracles and I will become your living miracle. I'll win the Olympics. I will be that miracle for not only myself but for all the children and people that don't believe their life is worth anything."

She broke into tears. "Just let him live, God. I promise, I promise..."

The shadows had grown long and the sky dark when one of the attendants finally located Naomi still in the church.

"Naomi," the young man said in hushed tones.

Her eyes stared straight ahead, afraid to move, afraid to face the truth.

"We've been looking all over for you."

Naomi braced herself for the bad news. "I'm sorry," she croaked. "I didn't mean to make your job harder. I just had to be alone...and Purnell..." She hung her head as a new well of tears enveloped her. She shook with the force of her feelings, but she made herself ask the question she feared the answer to.

"Have we gotten any news from the hospital?"

The young attendant glowed.

"Purnell's gonna be all right. That's what I came to tell you! He has a concussion, and they're watching him overnight to just make sure he's okay, but there's nothing long-lasting that they can see."

Naomi looked at him with an open mouth. "He's going to be okay?"

The man nodded. "They say miracles happen on a blue moon – so I guess this is that blue moon."

Naomi looked at the man oddly as her realities began to cross and tangle.

"Yes," she said with the realization of the magic that had occurred. "Especially when it's on Christmas."

"Especially on Christmas," he agreed.

Naomi looked back up at the cross which was suddenly illuminated by the rising of that very full moon. It shone through the stained glass in a beautiful, splintered, abstract version of itself, and for a moment, Naomi could swear God was winking at her.

Chapter 47

Samantha sat on the couch with her shoulder bandaged up, but peace in her heart. "I'll be home for Christmas" was playing, and she watched the blinking tree lights in a happy daze.

She felt safe and at home. Though in all honesty, she had neither. She couldn't remember the last time she had seen Tommy and Trulie so happy and relaxed.

Samantha choked back reality. Estelle had left in a fit, but her threat to contact Samantha's father still hung like a guillotine in Sam's mind. She wouldn't put anything past a woman like Estelle.

Despite the Henderson's warm welcome to stay a few days, Sam knew she had to get the kids out and get moving soon. They couldn't stay here forever in the protective clutches of Harold's family, as much as she wanted them to.

Samantha gave a deep sigh and looked at the clock. It was nine o'clock. Way past Trulie's bedtime. She was about to take her outside into the cold night, and then where?

Sam struggled to stand. "I guess we should get going."

Everyone stopped talking and looked up at Samantha. Mrs. Henderson stood too. She ordered everyone out of the room.

"There's pie in the kitchen. You all go and see to it. I need some alone time with Samantha."

The group filed out as commanded.

Mrs. Henderson came over and took both of Samantha's hands gently.

"I overheard your conversation with Estelle, and I think you're completely right. I think she's using my son, and I'm going to make sure Harold gets that DNA test before he gets roped into a life of unhappiness."

Samantha looked up at her and nodded. "He deserves better."

Mrs. Henderson looked at her with love. "He certainly does."

Mrs. Henderson brought her shirt cuff to her eye and wiped away a stray tear.
"So what's your plan, Samantha?"

Sam looked at her blankly. "I'm going to take the kids to another city maybe, in Ohio. It's not too far. I heard it's nice and they have good schools."

Mrs. Henderson reached out a kind hand and stopped her. "At least can I have Harold drop you somewhere?" She started to cry in spite of her strong desire not to.

"Look at me, now I'm blubbering."

"I'm so sorry. I never meant to cause any problems," Sam said earnestly.

Mrs. Henderson held up her hand.

"Darling, you have no reason to ask for forgiveness. I am so happy that you're all right, and I am also so very grateful that Estelle has exposed herself for who she truly is. My husband and I have never liked her for Harold. He doesn't seem happy with her, and she doesn't seem to have love for anyone but herself. But after witnessing what she just did, I cannot in good faith..."

She brought a hand to her throat as if it were difficult to communicate.

"When you have a child, you'll know, Samantha. You just want what's best for them. I want Harold to be happy. I was willing to accept Estelle if that's who he truly loved, but now..." She shook her head. "I cannot in all good faith spend my hard earned money to send my son on a honeymoon to Hawaii with a woman I think is a monster!"

She nearly shook with the force of her feelings.

"I can't choose what Harold's going to do, darling, but I can choose what I'm going to do."

With that she went to her desk and returned with a manila envelope that was stuffed full and handed it to Samantha.

Samantha raised her brows in surprise.

"What is this?"

"It's $30,000 that I was saving as a gift for Estelle and Harold's wedding gift. Now it's a gift to you. I took the liberty of looking up flights to Los Angeles."

Samantha gasped.

Mrs. Henderson stopped. "That's where you had been planning to go, right?"

Sam nodded. "I wanted to try acting for real…" Sam paused. That dream had died so long ago, and now it was rearing up again.

Sam looked down at the money. Acting had always been how she escaped her life, and now it was here to help again. She'd have the shot at the life she'd always dreamed of. The plane to LA took off in three hours, this was her chance to leave her father, and all the worries of her other life behind forever.

She just prayed that Harold would still be the man she shared it with.

Mrs. Henderson cupped her chin and tilted her eyes to meet hers. "Listen to me, Samantha. You have specialness in you. You might not see it, but I do. Consider it a loan, if it makes you feel better. Just promise me you'll get far away from your father and go – go become rich and famous! Then please save my son from a life of misery and gosh darn dental sales!" She wiped a tear away, and smiled.

"If you think it's best for you and the kids, take them too, but I'm still offering to take great care of the children, just until you're ready for them to come meet you."

Sam opened her mouth to argue.

"You need the money... and the kids need a safe secure place to grow up. Go be you. Go do something just for you Samantha. Who knows what could happen? It's Christmas, and miracles happen in the darndest way..."

Sam thought of the joy and ease she'd seen on the children's faces and, despite it breaking her heart, knew Mrs. Henderson was right. They would be happy here with them. They would have a chance at a great life at least. Her life was still up in the air. What could she really offer them that was better than living with the Henderson's?

"Just say yes, Samantha," Mrs. Henderson said lovingly. "I'm offering you a chance at a new life."

Sam nodded, sadly acknowledging the truth they both were forced to admit.

Chapter 48

The food and fun continued into the night, and then the dancing began.

Macy had no idea that people had this much fun on Christmas. She'd been invited to friends' holiday parties and stayed briefly, but she never witnessed the joy and true happiness these people seemed to share.

Summer Landers walked over and smiled broadly at her. "It sure is nice to meet you, Macy. We've all heard a lot about you for years. Maybe you can tell me what New York City's like. I've always wondered..." Summer's voice trailed off with wonder.

Macy thought about it. Compared to here, it was lifeless and full of shallow pursuits. What she said was, "It's nice... it's busy, and there are a lot of lights."

Macy started laughing. "I don't mean to make it sound so bad, except, well..." She looked over at Conner and her mother and all the wonderful people that were gathered in this room to celebrate.

"It's just nothing like this. This is what matters: family, home, and people that care about you."

Summer looked at her with understanding in her large liquid blue eyes.

"I think you need to come back and visit more often, Macy."

"I hope so, Summer," Macy said with true conviction.

Macy caught Conner staring at her and felt that familiar blush creeping up. Summer looked at her with a knowing look.

"Maybe you have more reasons to come back than you think?"

Good grief, Macy wanted to sink into the floor. Was it that obvious to everyone that she was head over heels in love with Conner?

She caught her breath at the revelation of her heart.

Without a shadow of a doubt she loved Conner Anderson.

Suddenly Conner was at her side, gazing at her with those sexy gray eyes that seemed to dance in the twinkly lights of the tree. Macy studied her feet.

Summer looked back and forth between the two of them. "See you later, guys. I'm going to go check and see if my mother needs any help." She slinked away with a wry smile.

Macy couldn't help but laugh. Conner wanted to know what was so funny. Macy shrugged. "I just think people in Kissing Bridge are really trying to fix me up with you."

"So is it working?" he asked casually, but his easiness belied a serious tone.

Macy wanted to tell him the truth of her heart, but what would it matter? All of this was about to be gone. They only had that moment.

She deflected.

"Did you bring Toulouse?"

Conner broke into laughter. "Not going too deep are you, Macy Kennedy? Just want to swim in the shallow waters, avoid feeling anything?"

"Stop sounding like my therapist," she chided.

"Well, I am a counselor."

"Let's just focus on the kitten."

Together they disappeared to fetch the big surprise. When they came back, Macy had a mischievous look on her face and Conner had a box in his hands.

"Mom," Macy announced. "I have one more gift for you."

Her mother stopped dancing with the neighbor and brushed her hair off her face. She came over and looked at the box curiously.

"That's for me?"

Macy nodded, and Conner gave her a conspiratorial wink. There was a rustling inside the box, and Macy's mom stepped back.

A tiny paw stuck out from one of the holes.

Macy smiled as the revelation of what it was came over her mother's face like sunshine.

They opened it up and Macy's mom pulled out Toulouse for all to see. Everybody clapped. They circled around to play with the new kitty.

Mrs. Kennedy beamed at her daughter incredulously. "Just what I wanted. How did you know?!"

Macy shrugged. "Seemed like you needed, well...Toulouse."

Macy's mom played with Toulouse's paw and the kitty nose butted her with affection.

Macy tried to take a mental picture of this moment so she could engrave it in her memory forever.

Conner's hand touched her shoulder. He rubbed her skin with his strong fingers in a very sexy way. She sucked in her breath, warmed by his nearness, but right now, she had to find those Landers sisters.

Macy located Carol and Ethel Landers in the kitchen, they were washing and drying dishes together and laughing.

She walked up next to Carol, and grabbed an extra towel and started helping dry the stack of dishes without speaking.

The sisters stopped talking and looked at her.

Macy cleared her throat.

"Look, the other day my mom – well she had a pain by her left side. And well, I don't know when I'll see her again…"

Carol and Ethel looked at each other.

Macy stammered on.

"I'm worried about her, and she doesn't seem open to going to see the doctor."

Ethel nodded. "She's stubborn about that for sure."

Carol concurred with a bob from her flaming red beehive.

Macy looked at them both. She had no idea if she was dreaming, or if they really had an enchanted recipe book, but right now she really needed their help.

Magical cookies or not.

"Will you promise me you'll make her go to the doctor?" Macy pleaded. "I know I can trust you."

Ethel looked her straight in the eye. "I promise, Macy. I will help get her there. I'll be a big pain in the butt."

Macy let out a short, thankful laugh. She knew Ethel well enough now to know, *she would be.*

Carol put down her rag and hugged Macy tight.

"And I will make her go to the doctor if I have to drag her skinny body myself. I'd do anything to help you and your mother. I hope you believe that now."

Macy nodded.

"I do." Macy said. "You're true friends. That's why I'm asking."

Ethel wiped away a tear and came over and joined in on their hug.

Macy squeezed them both tight and tears glistening in her eyes. "Thank you, Carol. Thank you, Ethel. From the bottom of my heart."

Macy rejoined the festive group in the front room and looked at the clock in agony. It was almost 11:00 p.m. This was her time to be with her mom.

Macy shuddered with the ghost of Christmas present. She knew that the next time she saw her mother that she would be cold, in a cheap wooden coffin, and all these people that loved her so much would be there to say goodbye.

Macy reluctantly looked back up at the clock, her new nemesis. The cookies had said that the do over lasted only until Christmas. After midnight, Christmas would be over.

She had been trying to stay as close to her mother as possible, and whenever they had spare moments, they had spent their time painting and just sharing each other's company.

She reached over and squeezed her mother's hand. She couldn't change the future or destiny, but at least this time, she wouldn't have any regrets.

Conner was smiling from across the room in a way that made her legs go weak.

But she hadn't counted on having regrets over this man.

Conner walked up to her.

"May I have this dance?"

He held out his hand to hers. "I think the party is wrapping up, and I haven't gotten a chance to dance with the most beautiful woman here. Not to mention how amazing you look in your red dress."

Macy blushed. She had bought herself a new dress just for the dinner today, and she had hoped he'd approve.

Soon they were dancing, and Conner spun her lightly around the room and held her close. She put her head on his shoulder and watched the party spin around her like a happy mirage.

She battled with herself over admitting the whole truth. That just like Cinderella's pumpkin, she was about to go poof.

As if reading her thoughts, Conner wrapped his arms around her closer. Macy adored being close to him, even if it couldn't last forever.

Conner's voice was a low rumble. "I'm just going to say it before you run off and I don't get the chance. I'm falling for you, Macy Kennedy, and if there's any way I can talk you into staying here in Kissing Bridge...would you give me an idea of what that might be?"

Macy's heart lurched. "Oh, Conner." If he only knew how futile it was.

He cast his eyes away at her blank response. "Well, if you don't feel the same way, I understand. I mean, maybe this is too small town for a big city girl like you... but, Macy, if you ever get tired of New York City, you will come look me up, won't you?'

Conner pulled away reluctantly and searched her eyes for answers.

Even though in her heart she knew that this was a fairytale that could never come true, Macy reached up and wrapped her arms around him tight, then kissed him long and deep and hard in answer to his question.

All the time she thought true love was a bunch of baloney, and now here she was, understanding exactly what people meant when they talked about soulmates.

Carol Landers appeared and touched Macy on the shoulder, waking her from her dream. Macy turned to her touch, and she said gently,

"It's time to go, Macy."

From the corner of her eye, Macy caught her mother's warm eyes smiling at her. Macy lifted her hand to her to say goodbye, and opened her mouth to ask for just one more minute, and suddenly she was hit with a beam of light.

Chapter 49

Samantha huddled with her brother and sister holding each of their hands. She looked into Tommy's green eyes, so much like hers, and ruffled his carrot mop.

"As soon as I'm settled in California, I'm going to get a big house and you both are going to come live with me. How does that sound?"

Tommy looked up. "You mean Malibu?"

Sam laughed a lovely tinkling sound.

"Sure Malibu! Why not think big!! She squeezed both their hands.

Trulie looked at her "Sam-Sam, Sam-Sam."

Samantha gathered her in closer, and sniffed hard to stop the tears that were threatening to fall.

She couldn't let them see how worried she was, but also how relieved she was to know that under the Henderson's roof they would be loved and taken care of; and most of all safe.

Harold waited patiently at the doorway with his coat and boots on. Samantha looked up at him and he smiled sadly. "I'm afraid we have to leave if you want to make that flight Sam."

Samantha's gaze flickered over to the ticking clock and she squeezed her eyes shut. This was the moment, her final choice to get it right, or not. She either left or she didn't.

Samantha pulled Tommy to her one more time, and hugged him tight. "As soon as I get my first job, I'm getting you a cell phone so we can talk everyday okay?"

Tommy's eyes widened. "Really a cell phone?"

Sam nodded. "With your own number." She could tell he was trying not to cry, and then he spun around and ran over to the Christmas tree and got involved in his new Lego set to hide his vulnerability.

Sam looked after her younger brother. She was making the right choice for him and Trulie. Sam picked up Trulie and hugged her tight. She wrapped her little pink bunny blanket around her and kissed her face all over. "I love you so much baby girl. I'll see you soon. Mrs. Henderson said she'd make you some cereal. Would you like that?"

Trulie's eyes opened up wide at the mention of food. "Siri-yo," she said in her little baby voice. They all started laughing.

Mrs. Henderson came over and Sam gently put Trulie into her arms. They looked into each other's eyes.

"Thank you," Sam said.

Mrs. Henderson kissed her on the cheek and smiled. "I promise we'll take good care of them both until you're ready."

Sam nodded. She cast her eyes around the lovely home once more, burning the memory of the precious moment into her mind. She looked at Harold and headed for the door with a heavy heart.

There was nothing left to say but goodbye. Even if she didn't get on the plane to Los Angeles, the clock would strike twelve and Christmas would be over. She'd pop back to where she came from, maybe.

Samantha thought how sad it was that you never really knew when you'd run out of time with the people you love in life. She was just going to love them with all her heart, as if it were the last time.

Chapter 50
The Present

The doorbell rang, and Macy gently removed Toulouse from her lap. As usual, her red sweater was stuck with little Toulouse yellow and white hairs. She picked a couple hairs off of her embroidered Santa's head near her shoulder and went to answer the door.

Carol Landers was there.

Carol had a big gift basket in her hand and the only thing Macy could see was her towering red beehive that rose almost to the ceiling.

"Hello, Macy! Merry Christmas." She called from behind her package.

"Carol! Merry Christmas! Let me help you with that." Macy reached out and took the gift basket from her hand. "Oh goodness, you've outdone yourself. This is amazing! How kind of you to come."

Macy peered in through the plastic surrounding the basket at the plethora of baked goods that the Landers sisters were famous for.

Inside, the home was warm and cozy. A fire blazed and the lilting sounds of Bing Crosby's "White Christmas" filled the room.

Toulouse came up and wrapped himself around Carol's leg in welcome. She scooped the kitty up and gave him a quick peck on the nose.

"The girls are in the kitchen," Macy said. "Can I get you something to drink? I have to be honest; we've already started with some Baileys in our coffee. It is Christmas, after all!"

Carol's eyebrow rose and she laughed a deep, hearty sound. "It certainly is, and I've already been to church this morning, so let the celebration begin!"

Macy patted her on the back with affection and ushered her into the dining room next to the kitchen.

Samantha and Naomi were busy making enough breakfast food for an army. Multiple loafs of bread were out – two toasters going strong and three cast iron pans of bacon sizzling. Samantha was chastising Naomi. "You're the health nut; shouldn't we be baking the bacon instead of frying it?"

They stopped when Carol and Macy entered.

Macy gestured to them. "Carol, you've met my friends Samantha and Naomi."

Carol smiled. "Hello again."

Samantha wiped her hands and came over and hugged Carol. "Merry Christmas."

"So," Carol began slowly as she glanced about Macy's mom's home. The whole house was dripping with decorations, and it looked as if Santa himself lived there. "It looks like quite the Christmas brunch you're putting together here; you must have some hearty appetites."

Naomi laughed. "No, it's not all for us. We have a couple guests and a whole lotta family! Thankfully the rest of the gang is busy skiing while we make the feast."

Samantha nudged her back and winked at Carol. "To be honest, we offered to make the brunch so we could have some girl time alone."

Macy poured a cup of coffee for the newcomer. "Baileys or no in your coffee?"

"Baileys of course," Carol said as she looked at the happy, easy camaraderie between the girls. Pride seemed to twinkle in her eye.

"So I know you've been friends a long time...but I never did hear how you all met."

Macy opened her mouth, and then Sam cut in.

"It was just before Christmas, on a blue moon just like this year!"

Macy looked at her. "What's that saying about once in a blue moon?"

Samantha screwed her face up in thought. "Magic happens?"

Macy hummed. "Yeah, or miracles? Okay, sorry, go on, Sammy."

Sam's mouth spread wide in her million-dollar smile.

"I was in Manhattan for the Emmys –it was my first win for 'Our House.'"

Carol nodded. "Oh, I'm a big fan. I thought I recognized that beautiful face of yours from somewhere."

No longer did Sam wear any scars from the pain she had known in her youth or past life. Her face was perfect, flawless, and now, famous as well.

"Thank you very much."

Samantha said as she brought over the carafe of coffee and set it on the table. "But it was so strange and coincidental how we ended up going to Macy's art show! We were waiting for a table at La Palma for dinner –you know how New York can be, waiting for a good restaurant?"

Carol did. She nodded. The story went on. "Well, there was a big art exhibit going on next to the restaurant, so we decided to pop in and check out this new up and coming artist Harold had heard about."

Naomi clapped her hands eager to join in. "And I had just finished a book signing down the street for 'Live the Golden Life.'"

Carol raised an eyebrow. "So you're an author?

Naomi waved her off. "By default! I'm an Olympic gold medal winner in track, and I somehow ended up writing a bestseller about my personal struggle and story of inspiration. I never expected my little book to take off the way it did!"

Carol nodded in awe. "How fabulous; a real Olympian and an actress right here in our little town! Macy, you didn't tell me your friends were famous!"

The girls beamed at each other with real affection. "I'd love to hear more," Carol urged.

Naomi continued. "Anyway, my husband, Purnell, had been waiting for me for hours, God bless him. The book signing went overtime, but I couldn't deny all those kids that had waited…When I finally finished, he told me I had to come see something before we went back to our hotel. I was exhausted but somehow I let him drag me into this crowded art event – and it was Macy's!"

Carol turned to Macy. "Well, isn't that a coincidence."

Macy whistled as if to say, "Right?" She elaborated. "That whole night was like a dream. I was so nervous. It was my first big art show and all the top critics were there. I was selling pieces left and right, and to tell you the truth, I was in a bit of shock."

Carol could understand. "So you all met there –at your grand art opening in New York City?"

Macy nodded. "But I still think it was destiny that brought us together."

Carol took a sip of her drink. "You don't say."

Macy smiled. "It was as if it was meant to be. Do you ever believe in things like that, Carol? My mom must have brainwashed me with her spiritual perspective towards everything! But still, it just seems that fate had a hand to play in all of this."

Carol looked her dead in the eye. "Love and miracles happen all the time if you just believe they can."

Naomi turned off the skillets on the stove and joined them at the table. "I was ready to bolt–honestly–no offense, Macy. You know I love your art; I own three pieces. But I wasn't in the mood for a big event."

Naomi shook her head at the memory. "So Purnell literally drags me by the arm to see this picture that Macy had painted, and darn if one of those girls in the picture wasn't a spitting image of me! I couldn't believe it. Stopped me dead in my track shoes, I can tell you." She laughed. "And I looked good too!"

They all laughed. Naomi continued with a gleam in her eye at the memory. "It was not like any of her other paintings, either – which were amazing, there was no doubt that Macy was going to make her mark on the art scene, but this one was different. It was more realistic, like a photograph of time gone by. It was of a quaint home, and friends gathered around a table in celebration."

She gazed around the table. "In fact it looked a lot like this..." She trailed off.

Samantha picked up the story. "About that time my husband, Harold, showed up with the curator and they were trying to haggle over a price he would take for *the same exact painting*. But the curator said it wasn't for sale."

"I'll double the price –whatever it is..." Harold had said to him. "I have to have this for my wife! That woman in the picture is a spitting image of her!"

Samantha looked at the women gathered around the table. "Honestly, when

Harold wants something, there's no stopping him. He's the best agent in Hollywood, so he knows how to bargain, and right then, he was bent on buying that painting!"

Naomi cut in. "And so Harold and Purnell started this bidding war over Macy's painting."

"I came over to see what the uproar was about," said Samantha, "and that's when I saw the same painting. *It was me*...at the table with them." She looked at her friends. "It was an unbelievable likeness."

Macy finished the story. "That's when I came over, at the curator's request, to explain that the painting wasn't for sale at *any price* because it was too sentimental! I had painted it from one of my mother's original pencil sketches, and it was kind of my ode to her."

Macy looked at her dear friends across the table and reached out and took both of their hands. "We took one look at each other and it was as if destiny had already decided we needed to be friends."

They all smiled, and Carol Landers couldn't have been happier. She gazed around the lovely group of women now gathered at Macy's mom's old wooden table.

They were happy.

Carol took a big sigh, and her red beehive bobbed up and down with her deep breaths of satisfaction.

"So what's next for you then, Samantha?"

"I'm about to start this really fascinating movie actually about the *Butterfly Effect*. Time travel. Have you ever heard about it?"

Carol leaned in, interested. "Oh, do tell."

Chapter 51

Sam took a sip of coffee and looked around at her friends. "*The Butterfly Effect* is about how even our smallest choices can have far reaching effects in our lives. So something as simple as the flutter of a butterfly's wing can have an impact we may never know."

Macy frowned and shook her head. "Whoa, that's deep! I'm just trying to figure out when I should start setting the table, and if I should treat myself to one of these delicious cookies Carol brought."

The group laughed at the levity.

Macy held up a cut out cookie in the shape of a Christmas tree. "Do you think this will have far reaching effects?" she joked, as she popped it in her mouth.

They all laughed and Carol's eyes twinkled.

Suddenly, a ruckus could be heard outside the door and a mass of people came streaming in.

"Mom!" a young, pretty, blonde-haired girl yelled enthusiastically to her mother across the room. "I did my first jump on my snowboard!"

Samantha opened her mouth to object, when Harold slapped a mitten-clad hand over his daughter's face affectionately.

"It was a very small jump and I was right there with her!"

Samantha's fire died down. "Juliet, just be careful, you're still a beginner." She looked over at her twin boys who were busy taking off their hats and coats.

"And you two don't be instigating this dare devil behavior!"

Cody and Jordan smiled in unison and said, "Yes mom!" Then they high-fived each other over the jinx.

Cody waved to the group at the table. He had his father's facial structure but Samantha's unusual green eyes. "Sarah and Melanie went ice skating with Grandma and Grandpa Henderson so they'll be here soon."

Samantha smiled at her brood. "Well sit down we're almost ready with the food."

She and Macy walked into the kitchen hand in hand. They had come a long way together. But now, they had to finish up breakfast for the hoard of hungry people gathering at their Christmas table.

Macy turned the bacon over and Samantha started cracking the eggs into a big bowl. "I have a feeling we might need more eggs!"

A moment later, Naomi's crew trudged in the front door with their coats all speckled with new fallen snow. They were still shaking bits of it from their boots.

Purnell beamed at the gathered group.
"Merry Christmas everyone! He waved from the door. "I can attest from the lodge that the view was beautiful and I loved

watching everyone *else* risk their lives on those mountains." He laughed a hearty sound and came over and kissed his wife on the cheek.

"Hey beautiful."

"Hey handsome." Naomi smiled up at him with her almond-eyes glowing with love. Her son and his girlfriend hung up their coats and waved to the assembled group. "This is my son Derek, "Naomi said proudly, "He's my lawyer to be."

Derek ducked his head and made a face.

"Mom stop saying that to everyone." Naomi smiled at him. "And this is his girlfriend Deidra. Hopefully my daughter-in-law-to-be."

Derek rolled his eyes. "Mom…"

There was a light knock at the door, and Naomi got up. "I'll get it." She walked over to answer. It was someone she didn't know, but she did recognize those big green eyes.

She was a cute strawberry-blonde haired girl with an uncertain tone in her voice. "I'm sorry" she started, "I'm not sure if this is the right place...I'm looking for my sister?"

Naomi threw the door open. "Get in here girl you've got the right place! It's cold outside."

Samantha shot out from the kitchen like a bullet at the sound of her sister's voice. "Trulie! You made it!" She threw herself into her sister's arms and Trulie hugged her tight.

"Get comfortable and take off your coat." Samantha helped her younger sister remove her coat.

Macy came out from the kitchen and put a big plate of French toast on the table. "Welcome Trulie!" She beamed out to Sam's younger sister. "Its so nice to have you with us. What a glorious Christmas surprise!"

Trulie joined the group at the table and kissed her nephews and nieces with affection. Harold pulled out a chair for her.

"Great to see you Trulie."

"You too Harold. So wonderful to see you all."

Suddenly, Tommy poked his head in the door and his red hair was sprinkled white with snowflakes. "Hi everyone Merry Christmas! Sorry I'm late, but I couldn't drag myself off the mountain! Sammy you were right! Kissing Bridge is the best skiing I've had in years!"

Samantha ran over and hugged him tight. "Hey big sis." He hugged her back affectionately. "Merry Christmas Sammy."

She turned to the group. "This is my brother Tommy!"

Tommy came in and waved to the group of happy people seated around the table awaiting Christmas brunch. He hugged his younger sister warmly.

"Hey Trulie you made it! I'm so happy to see you. How's the hospital?"

"Busy. "She smiled. "How's owning your own business, Mr. Malibu?"

He laughed. "Better than working for anyone else!"

Carol Landers smiled at the handsome redhead with the easy smile." Oooh Malibu. I've heard it's lovely." Carol said.

Tommy nodded. "Oh yes, it's amazing. The minute I saw the ocean next to those mountains I knew I had to have it, so I bought a small piece – very small, and I just built on it from there."

Trulie smiled and teased her older brother. "Now we call him *Mr. Malibu*."

He waved it off. The group laughed with him. Samantha was all smiles. Her husband, her children, and her dear siblings were all together.

She glanced at Macy and Naomi and a past flicker of another time passed like a ghost. She shook it away, and concentrated on all of the many loved ones that had gathered together here in this adorable mountain town to celebrate Christmas together, and she felt truly blessed.

Chapter 52

There was a quick knock on the door, and then suddenly it banged open with a big gust of wind, and there stood Conner Anderson.

His large hunky frame filled the small doorway and he was laden down with so many bags of gifts you could barely see his cleft chin. "Sorry if I scared you all!" Conner boomed good-naturedly.

Macy jumped up and met him at the door. He bent over and kissed her adoringly. "How's my beautiful wife?"

Macy beamed up at his handsome grey flannel eyes with love glowing on her face. "Happier that you're here."

Conner set the gifts down and embraced his wife and gave her a long big kiss. "Merry Christmas Macy."

Macy felt as if she must be the luckiest woman in the world. How many times she had been heartbroken over fools? She had nearly given up on love altogether, but somehow she and Conner had found each other, in different places and against all odds.

"Do you mind putting these under the tree darling?" Conner asked. "I still have to grab some more packages from the truck."

Harold stood up. "You need some help Conner?"

Conner waved him off. "No Harold thanks man, please enjoy your breakfast. The snow is really coming down heavy now, and the walkway must be two feet deep. I've still got my snow boots on. I'm pretty sure I can get it all in one more trip."

Macy took all the presents out of the two big bags Conner had brought in and placed them under the tree. Toulouse jumped on them immediately and started pawing at the bows.

Macy laughed and scooped up the fat kitty and kissed him on his little pink nose. "You get to play with the wrapping paper *after they're opened,* Toulouse. I promise."

Macy placed a log on the fire and smiled. The moving notes of "Angels We Have Heard on High" rang through the house. Macy sighed. She couldn't be happier than she was right now.

She looked over at her friends and thought that nobody in the world could possibly be as blessed as she. A slight sliver of obligation ran through her as she realized she hadn't made it to church yet, but she stopped and looked up at the cross on her mother's wall and said a prayer of thanks.

This was the best Christmas she had ever had.

Chapter 53

Harold spotted Conner making his way back to the house with his hands full, and got up and opened the door for him.

The wind pushed a big gust of snow through the door, sending snowflakes fluttering through the room like bits of starlight. Conner strode in holding the best package of all.

He had Macy's mom cradled in his arms.

She was wearing a chic red pantsuit, a dashing pair of Chanel high heels, and a smile on her face.

"Merry Christmas, everyone!" She waved at the group gathered around her table from Conner's arms.

"You can put me down now, Conner."

Conner gently placed Mrs. Kennedy on her feet and she looked up triumphantly and patted her hair all done up in a pretty bun with a sprig of holly. "And maybe you should go get Ethel?"

Ethel arrived in that moment, and waved to the crowd. "I can walk my darn self. I know when to wear suitable shoes Lenora."

Macy came over and squeezed her mother with all her might. "Merry Christmas, Mom!"

"Merry Christmas, darling." She smiled at her daughter. She was gleaming with love and her dancing brown eyes were full of mischief.

Macy looked down at her feet and reprimanded her.

"Mom, you can't be wearing your Chanel shoes in this kind of weather; you're bound to get frostbite."

Her mom waved a hand. "Darling, I was not about to wear snow boots at Christmas Mass when my daughter gave me my first pair of fancy-schmancy designer shoes."

The table of friends started laughing.

Macy turned to them. "Don't egg her on! She hasn't taken those off since I gave them to her! I had to stop her from wearing them with her pajamas."

Her mother extended a single foot on display. "What do you think, Carol?" She twisted her foot side to side. "Don't I look all N-Y-C fancy now?"

Carol laughed. "That's one word for it!"

Ethel shook her head and took her coat off. "And I have the other one."

Harold pulled a chair out for each of them. "Come on, sit down ladies."

They both sat down and Macy's mom joined them. She marveled at the cookie display from the Landers.

"Have you ever seen anything so beautiful and delicious at the same time?" She examined the culinary art piece. "You really do make the best cookies, my friends, blue ribbon winners or not."

Carol patted her affectionately. "Oh, watch your words, Lenora!" she chided.

Macy's mom smiled. "I can tell you one thing for sure: if nothing else will bring you back to Kissing Bridge, these magical cookies will."

Macy caught her breath as if a chill had run through her, or a phantom memory that was there and then gone. Samantha met her eyes in understanding, and Naomi reached out and took Macy's hand.

Conner lifted his coffee cup to the group.

"I want to make a toast to all the friends and family that have gathered here today. I wish you all love, blessings, and most of all a very merry Christmas! Merry Christmas, everyone!"

They all held up their coffee cups and toasted. "Merry Christmas."

Macy's mom smiled at her and Macy's eyes caught hers.

"And to my dear daughter," her mother added, "who is truly the greatest gift I've ever had."

Carol smiled proudly as she looked around the joyous table of family and friends gathered together for the holy celebration.

She raised her cup of coffee in toast and winked at Macy's mom.

"Merry Christmas, my dear friend," she said sincerely. "Merry Christmas to you all."

The End.

Here is a sneak peak excerpt!

Chapter 1

"WHAT IS THIS?" I screamed to no one, because I was the only person crazy enough to be outside in this snowstorm.

The driving snow gusts whipped me in the face, and I regretted that I was too vain to wear one of those face sweaters that make you look like a hoodlum.

I slid my backpack off and threw it on top of the snow, ready to do battle. I wiggled the post of the *For Sale sign* on our lawn back and forth and attempted to unleash it from the ice that had formed around the base. I couldn't believe someone would play a joke like this—especially around Christmas.

I scanned the neighborhood for possible offenders before spotting Mr. Aikens through the sheets of white, shoveling his car out of his driveway next door. He looked innocent enough. Even if he didn't donate to my *Save the Trees Campaign.*

I waved. He waved back and shouted, "Hey, Allie. I spotted you down the block. Was that an Uber car you got out of?"

I gritted my teeth and looked back over my shoulder at my drop off point. I concocted a little fib because I couldn't tell Mr. Aikens the truth, or he'd blab it to my father for sure. They played bocce ball every Wednesday.

I swear those older men gossip more than my girlfriends.

"No, of course not. Ex-Boyfriend—boyfriend's car…"

I still hadn't gotten used to the *ex* part, although I should have it tattooed on my forehead by now.

"Go out with me, and I promise you'll leave me for someone better."

My ex, Shane, had *officially* left me two years ago, one day after my mother lost her long battle with cancer. I still hadn't the heart to tell my dad that Shane had left me when I needed him most. I kept saying he was busy. It was hard enough for me to deal with the fact he had bailed on me at the worst time of my life. At twenty-seven, I wasn't old enough to be jaded, but honestly, I was scarred.

I continued my struggle with the unwanted sign and wondered again who had the nerve to put up a *For Sale* sign in our yard? I had heard prices had been going up on the Jersey Shore, so maybe some overly zealous realtor made a mistake?

I called out through the whistling snow flurries. "Mr. Aikens, by any chance do you know who put this sign up?"

Mr. Aikens looked over with a tilt of his head to study the oddity. "Nope."

Humph. Now I was officially annoyed. I finally got on both sides of the darn sign and tugged straight up with all my force. It gave loose suddenly, of course, with my last thrust and sent me flying across the yard a good three feet. I landed with a thud on my back and the stupid sign on top of me. I wrestled it off and dusted off the snow.

"Need help?' Mr. Aikens offered now.

"No, no, I got it, thanks."

I stood up and gathered my sense of humor, and my backpack. If I had seen anyone else do this, I would have laughed my butt off. Since it was me, I wasn't as amused.

"Well, Merry Christmas to you, Allie." Mr. Aikens smiled. "You tell your father hello for me."

"I will. Merry Christmas to you and Mrs. Aikens."

I waved goodbye as I started the trudge up our tundra-like driveway with the hated sign tucked under my arm. When I found out who did this, they were going to hear it from me.

I tossed the offensive sign in the garage and shut the door. It was time to lie to my father. He'd ask me where Shane was, and I'd say I took the bus because Shane was busy– *again.*

The honest to goodness truth is, *I did take Uber.* I'm broke as heck, but I couldn't deal with the train-bus-train combo I'd have to endure. Christmas was always tough emotionally since mom passed, and I didn't need to freak out over a little Uber.

It's all Shane's fault, anyway, as far as I'm concerned. He's the one who talked me into college in the city–how romantic—driving together and forever after. All of those were lies! He left me for an Icelandic blonde intern at the dean's office! He said she was polished and perfect and he had fallen in love by mistake.

By mistake?

To add insult to injury, he had also stopped driving me to college at the request of Ms. Sweden. This is why I had to deal with the dreaded bus-train combo and ultimately be lying to my father and my neighbor right now.

This is why I hate men.

You give them everything, and then they disappear like a leech full of blood that falls off when it's done using you.

That is why if this were a real love story, my true love would be Uber. Uber has never let me down. Uber is always there for me. Uber does not prefer Icelandic blondes. I'm no Einstein, but I know that *falling in love with an inanimate object is far safer than falling in love with a man.*

Chapter 2

Unfortunately, my affair with Uber is an unrequited love since my family is in the car service business. Sadly, the company profits from Archer Premier Transport had been cut in half due to the arrival of my perfect Uberian love. The mega driving service had, without a doubt, revolutionized travel in the modern world.

I opened the side door, and Christmas music welcomed me in. The archway had been newly lit with twinkly lights and mistletoe. My stomach did that pit-drop thing it does whenever I feel something. I realized it was the decorations.

We had always done them together, but now Dad must have put them up for me. I took a deep breath. Christmas had a way of bringing up all the memories people tried to shut away.

Dad was in the middle of stirring something in a big pot when I came into the kitchen. I guessed it was Hungarian goulash, which was his signature and only complicated dish.

He had a defeated slump to his stirring. I kissed him on the cheek and threw my purse on the chair, which elicited a big, resentful *meow!*

My cat, Piewacket, leapt off the chair and gave me the evil cat-eye. It's not my fault her brown-toned fur blends in with all the colonial furniture! I've sat on her numerous times. I should get her a white collar.

"Sorry, Pie," I called over. She resent-meowed back at me and sashayed out of the room.

I pulled off my snowcap and ran my hands through my tangle of mousy hair. It was flat at the top where my cap has crushed it, and no amount of fluffing was rectifying that today.

"Dad, did you know someone put up a *For Sale* sign on the lawn?"

He stopped stirring and stared out the window at the falling snow.

"Dad–did you hear me?" I asked. He finally looked at me and shook his head. Uh oh. His eyes were *navy tone.*

Dad is the easiest person to read. He has amazing blue eyes, which change like a mood ring. His eyes can go from joyous royal blue to peaceful cerulean blue, to serious deep blue to this–*crisis* navy blue color they were now.

"Dad, what's wrong?"

"I didn't want to worry you, Allie." I felt this ominous cloud hit me. He put down the ladle and hung his head.

"After your mom got sick, I leveraged everything we had to help with the hospital bills, but it wasn't enough on any account…" He paused. "We're…I'm losing the house."

I froze.

"Wait –are you saying *you* put the *For Sale* sign up?"

He nodded sadly.

I threw my hands up. "You have got to be kidding me! I can't believe you'd even think about this!"

"I have no choice. I'm sorry, Allie. We have to sell or they'll foreclose on it. If I sell now while the area is hot, maybe I can save some of my investment and the business."

"You leveraged Archer Premier as well?"

He nodded.

I tried to make sense of this, but it was shocking. Dad had never mentioned money problems before. Sure, I knew things had been tight because of the medical bills, but I had no idea it had gotten so bad.

"Dad, we can't sell Mom's house!

A tear sprang to his eyes. "I've been trying to save it, honey. I just haven't been able to catch up. This is my last resort."

I looked around the living room I knew like the back of my hand. The sunflower stencils Mom and I had done…the penciled graph on the wall of me growing, or not–I had hoped for more than my five-foot-three but, alas, it was not to be. The fake Christmas tree we'd had as long as I could remember…I loved this house. I had planned to live here for the rest of my life.

I began to hyperventilate, which is my go-to panic attack coping mechanism.
Dad came over and wrapped his beefy arms around me.

"Breathe, Allie. Breathe."

I sucked in deep breaths, and I sniffed in his Old Spice cologne that Mom had gotten for him every year at Christmas. I wondered if he was running out. Two years now. Mental note—*get more Old Spice*. Never thought I'd say that.

"Mr. Somerset mentioned the Carriage House being available. He's very generous. Of course, it's much farther from the college…"

"There is no way we are taking charity from the Somersets, Dad. I hate them." I pulled back and Betty-Booped him with my own big, blue-eyed look that meant I was serious.

"Dad, I thought the business was doing fine. You never mentioned…"

"People don't need private cars anymore; they take Uber. Thankfully we have the Somersets, or we would go under just like all the other car services."

I swallowed my guilt and promised myself I would delete my Uber app as soon as I was alone.

"What can we do now? I want to help."

He looked me in the face, and a half-smile lifted the side of his full lips that didn't quite make it to his eyes. "We can move on, darling. A house is not home–*a home is where the heart is…"*

I repeated the words with him.

My mother had always said that. But the only thing we had left to show she had lived, loved, and made a place for her heart was right here. *I'd be darned if I ever let this house go.*

I wiped away a tear with an irritating swipe of the hand. "I'll put off finishing college. I can get a full-time job or work with you–whatever it takes. How much do we need to save the house?"

He let out a deep huff of defeat. "Two hundred thousand dollars."

"Two hundred thousand dollars?" I reeled.

He nodded.

"Did you just say two hundred thousand dollars?" Full Betty-Boop eyes now.

"Yep, that's right. Two hundred thousand dollars."

"Two hundred thousand dollars!" My heart sank. The staggering sum deflated my optimism like a prick to a balloon. Impossible.

I squeezed my eyes tight. I worked part time as a waitress at the Caddy Shack, but it barely paid for my books and mounting college bills. How the heck was I going to help find two hundred thousand dollars?

Two hundred thousand dollars.
Two hundred thousand dollars.
Two hundred thousand dollars.

I wracked my brains. How does one get money like that when they need it?

Chapter 3

"I assume you tried to leverage the house—" I began.

Dad went back to stirring the goulash. "I've taken out three loans on the house, honey. We're loaned out."

"Anything we can take out of Archer Transport?"

He glanced at me with his guilt royal blue orbs. "As much as I could without losing it."

I let out my breath. I was not overly smart, and this was beyond my thinking capacity. I was running out of options.

"Do we have any rich friends I don't know about?" I asked with hope.

Dad shook his head. "Not that I know of."

"What about in the movies when those gamblers get into trouble? They always find some seedy guy to loan them money. I wonder how they go about getting two hundred thousand dollars?"

Dad shrugged. "Not sure how to go about soliciting the mob."

I made a mental note to ask the cook at work, Frankie Musso, if he had any connects. He always bragged about being from Sicily. I wondered if inquiring about mob connections would be considered offensive. Not that I care about civilities now.

Still, it was a loan. I would have to pay the mob back sometime. I wondered what the penalty would be if you didn't pay back the mob. Would they kill me, or maybe just break my leg so I could pay them later? Two hundred thousand dollars for a broken leg seemed fair.

I imagined myself with a broken leg taking one for the team. It wouldn't be pleasant, but I wasn't an athlete or anything, so I could deal with a hobble for six months until it healed.

I did wonder how exactly they would go about the process of breaking my leg, though. Would they shoot it with a gun, or just hit my poor kneecap with a big bat? The mob guys on TV seemed to use bats a lot. Then again, who's to say they'd stop at one leg?

Maybe two hundred thousand dollars with no payback would mean a double leg breaking. I looked down at my innocent legs and rubbed them. I suddenly had more appreciation for limbs.

I needed some creative way to get the two hundred grand—*without* needing to pay it back.

A college pal, Tammy Hines, put her virginity up for sale to the highest bidder on Facebook to pay for her tuition.

I wondered what that total had come to and if Tammie had shared it in her Saturday morning confessional at St. Paul's. Not sure how many rosaries that would come to. Maybe that's why I hadn't seen her lately.

I'd have to call her later in any case because desperate times called for desperate measures– and I liked my legs.

A happy Christmas song came on in the background and I choked up. This was so messed up. Christmas had always been my favorite time of year. We made cookies and homemade gifts for each other like we were in some Rockwell sketch. Now everything had a gray veil over it, like the whole photo album of memories had been switched to monotones.

Dad spooned goulash into Christmas bowls decorated with bells and elves. He put them on the table and plopped down beside me. The spicy stew wafted up and my stomach grumbled. I blew on my goulash and took a big spoonful.

"Good?" he queried.

I smiled. "Awesome as usual."

Dad grew the tomatoes himself in the back office, along with multiple herbs during the winter months. It was his passion. I could taste a hint of the basil and its fresh bite against the heavier flavors.

"Good job with the lemon basil–nice touch."

He glowed and took another spoonful.

I glanced around the kitchen and the twinkly lights that rimmed the ceiling—we pulled them out every year during the holidays. We lived a middle-income, cozy life, and I had always been fine with that. Now for the first time I wanted more. I wanted that two hundred grand.

"Dad, I just don't get the world! We're good people with good morals, how come we aren't getting rewarded for it?'

"We have each other …"

"I know, and I'm grateful, but I'm talking about money! How come all of the mean people have all the money?"

He let out his breath as he added some pepper to his goulash. "You can't change the world, Allie."

I cocked my head to the side. I'd given up on men, but I wasn't about to give up on the world. I still had hope that if I threw all my energy into helping the world, I'd live a life well lived. Maybe get a park dedicated to me with my name on it. Better yet, buy the rainforest in the Amazon and protect it forever. I took in a deep breath. It did sound impossible.

"Maybe I'll double down on the scratch offs and get lucky. I brought you some home by the way—they're in my backpack."

Dad's eyebrows rose and he got up from the table. He just loved his scratch offs.

"They're in the side pocket," I called over.

He fished them out and held them up triumphantly.

"Thanks, honey. Maybe we'll get lucky."

He brought them back to the table and pulled out his lucky quarter and got scratching.

"I don't know, maybe I should think outside the box – what would I do if I wasn't a nice Catholic girl?"

Dad looked up from rubbing off the scratch ticket. "You mean like be a stripper?"

"What? No! I'm saying we're not going to lose this place. Okay? I don't know how, but I'll figure it out."

Dad scratched off the last lotto tickets and shook his head. "Better luck next time."

I pondered my spoonful of goulash and wondered when our *next time* would come.

Chapter 4

"I saw on TV that a bunch of people got arrested in a protest in front of the Somerset building–please tell me you weren't there." My dad had his serious eyeshade going–azure.

My face flamed and I made a production of loving my goulash. "Yum!" I said instead of fibbing anymore.

Of course I was there. I organized the darn fair wage protest! Somerset Industries made a fortune and paid their workers less than other prominent companies in the area.

The truth was I had bumped straight into the heir to the Somerset Throne before the police pulled me away–with a warning.

I glanced at the clock. "You better get ready to go to the center, Dad–I put your Santa outfit on the hanger in the guest room. That tummy takes up a lot of room." I laughed.

Argument deflected.

Dad's phone chirped and he put a finger up and lowered his voice to his professional tone. I recognized the ring. Mr. Moneybags on the redline. "Hello, Mr. Somerset. Of course. Right away."

Chapter 5

I cleaned up our dishes and helped myself to some chocolate milk. The snowstorm outside looked like it had gone code red. I could barely see our birdbath in the backyard.

I cast a glance at Dad's serious expression as he paced and listened. Stupid Somersets. I hated them. They were everything I abhorred about humanity. They were also my family's benefactors in a way. Sigh.

The blue-blood Somerset's were THE SOMERSETS of Long Island's old money, and also owners of Somerset Enterprises. They had made their billions in multiple areas, but the most significant was in boxes.

They were the providers for Bamazon, and the online retail business kept going straight up along with their need for boxes.

The youngest Somerset, Devlin, had taken over the reins a bit ago and had been credited for steering the bulk of their assets into the box realm. As the world became more delivery orientated, the need for boxes had grown and grown, and with it, their fortune. They owned half of the trees in America and employed people all over the country.

The royal Somersets were also and had always been Dad's biggest client. He had chauffeured Mr. and Mrs. Somerset and their children since they were born. We had lived on the extensive property when I was a child back in the days when carriage houses still had a place in proper society. And until the spoiled Sissy Somerset decided that our home should be *her* art studio and we had to move.

In the end, the change had been the best thing for us. Dad bought us our own home here on the Jersey Shore, and we had started a new venture. As well as being the premier chauffeur for the Somersets and keeping their cars in order, Dad and Mom had invested in more cars over the years and started Archer Premier Transport.

Dad came back into the kitchen, looking troubled. I was afraid to ask.

He finally blew out his breath and released a short laugh. "Well, when it rains, it pours, doesn't it, darling? Or when it snows, it blizzards, in this case." He cut a glance at the snow-packed window.

I looked up from petting Piewacket, who was sprawled on my lap. "What did the Superior Somersets need from you *today?*" I said in my fake haughty voice.

"Mr. Somerset has decided he would like to go out–despite the conditions. I'm going to have to call the center and tell them I won't be there to play Santa tonight this year."

I sprang to my feet in battle mode, and Piewacket fell off my lap. She was beyond irritated with me again, but I didn't have time for her. There was no way the Somersets were ruining my mom's special holiday function she had started! It was a tradition!

Ooooh, it was sooooo typical of the Somersets to call last minute and ruin everything!

"Dad, no–just say no."

"It's okay, darling. I don't feel much up to ho-ho-hoing, anyway." The sadness in his eyes showed that wasn't the truth.

I put my hands on my hips. "No, no, no, no! The homeless center holiday party was so important to Mom. I know it's always been important to you too!"

I pointed out the window at the dire weather. "They've been issuing no driving warnings all over the news—they can call somebody else! Just say no, Dad."

Dad patted me on the back. "Yes, they can call somebody else, honey, but if they start calling another car service, or worse, Uber, I will lose my biggest client. I can't say no to the Somersets."

Another Christmas interrupted by those overindulged Somersets. How many holidays or special occasions were interrupted because the Somersets called?

"Dad, they don't care about other people. They don't care that maybe you were spending Christmas morning with your child or your sick wife, they just—"

"Allie, stop, darling. I appreciate the Somersets. They gave us a great life, and it's not their fault we lost your mother."

It was just too much. Mom gone, our home about to be lost–and the homeless center holiday party without their Santa? Maybe I couldn't change everything, but I could save Mom's legacy and a little child's dream at Christmas.

"Who called? Which one is it–the old man?"

Dad smiled. "No, he's been out of town for a long while now. It's Devlin."

Oh, of course. Devlin. Figures. Who goes out in the middle of a snowstorm anyway? Devlin Somerset, because the weather stops in his wake.

"Seriously, where does he need to go in this crazy blizzard?"

"Not for me to ask, darling. My job is to drive."

"Dad, just let me go drive him. I'll go take the spoiled brat where he needs to get dropped off. He's probably going to the 21 clubs, or a strip club, more likely, knowing Devlin."

I pushed on when my Dad hesitated. "You just said yourself we can't afford to lose the Somersets as clients. I'm home now, and I'm going to help, and I'm going to start by doing what Mom would've liked. You're going give out the toys tonight, and I'm going drive the self-centered brat."

Dad scratched his head and I rushed on.

"I've been driving for you practically since I could drive. I can certainly take Mr. Fancy-Pants around town or whatever he needs. He never even looks through the darn divider window; he probably won't even know it's not you!"

Dad laughed at that thought. Despite the fact his daughter refused to wear makeup or mess with her locks other than to pull them up in a ponytail–yours truly was a natural beauty. No thanks to me. I had Mom's long eyelashes framing blue eyes that snapped with life and fire. No, I'm sure Dad couldn't imagine anyone not seeing his daughter's natural beauty, but Devlin Somerset might be blind enough to his own narcissism that he wouldn't even notice. Dad seemed to consider it.

I pushed him toward the back room and the awaiting Santa Suit.

"Look—go to the center, and I'll meet you there. I'm sure I'll be back in a snap, and we'll celebrate together."

He seemed doubtful, but I was not about to leave the kids disappointed.

"Please, don't leave the kids hanging. You know how much they count on this—we might not be able to do anything about some things, but we can make a difference tonight. You know Mom would want you to be there."

Dad eyes softened –light blue. He knew I was right. Devlin rarely left the Upper East Side, so it was sure to be a quick ride.

"I wish I had somebody else—but with this blizzard coming and all the airports closed..." He looked doubtful, but I could see he was relenting.

"Of course, I always have their Rolls Royce Limo ready, so that's thankfully not an issue."
Dad's face clouded with doubt. "Are you sure...?"

I held out my hand. "Give me the address."
I wasn't taking no for an answer.

He inhaled deeply and reached in his pocket, producing the pickup location. He handed it over tentatively.

"Okay, darling. I have a uniform that should fit you. It won't be perfect." His brow furrowed.

"Don't worry, Dad. He won't even know it's me, and I'll be back before you can say jingle bells."

Chapter 6

I pulled the chauffeur cap over my piled-up hair and tucked in a stray lock. No matter how much I adjusted the overly big uniform, I still looked like Tom Hanks in *Big*.

The bellboy of the Chic Park Avenue Elite Apartments opened the side limo door as Devlin Somerset strode out of the glass entrance with a statuesque blonde bombshell gliding behind him.

I kept my head down as I glanced at the handsome man in the Gucci suit and elegant tweed coat draped over his shoulder as if he were an off-duty superhero.

Devlin Somerset was a chiseled work of man-art that was for sure. Even as a child, he had been overly cute. Now that he was grown, he was tall with imposing shoulders that made everything he wore an instant fashion statement.

I studied him in the side mirror as they approached. Everything about him screamed *rich*. He was tanned despite the weather, and his gray eyes were enough to make any girl go soft inside. He had graced the cover of GQ and been named the *World's Sexiest Man,* but I knew firsthand what a spoiled jerk he really was.

I cast my eyes down and pulled in my breath as Devlin and his date slipped into the back seat. If I were lucky, they'd never even notice I wasn't my father driving as usual.

I glanced briefly into the rearview mirror to see if I had been detected, but thankfully Devlin was caught up in his voluptuous platinum-haired bombshell in the back seat. She was kissing him as his hand ran up her leg like ice cream.

The bellboy opened the door and handed me an address. "Mr. Somerset will be vacationing at his family Ski Chalet in the mountains for a holiday. This is the address."

I nodded like I imagined my father would and looked at the paper with the address. My eyes widened.

Kissing Bridge–Vermont!

Vermont?!

Seriously?

My heart quickened. Vermont was five hours away! I took a deep breath, but my heart sank. I would never make it back in time for the holiday party tonight! I wanted to groan, but I was afraid Devlin might hear.

I considered my options while Devlin's face was busy buried in his date's massive bosoms. I really wanted to know how long he planned to STAY in Vermont. Gosh, darn it. Drivers drove. They didn't question their bosses' choices. I had promised Dad I would handle it.

I glanced out at the inclement weather, unsure of traversing dangerous mountain roads in a Rolls Royce limo with no tire bands. New York City streets were one thing, but the ski mountains of Vermont were an entirely different story.

There was a heavy rap on the dividing window and I jumped like a ninny.

"Let's get a move on, Charles, I'd rather not be caught in the blizzard on this side of the mountainside," Devlin said.

I groaned and put the Rolls into gear.

This is the end of the excerpt – get the book now right here
https://www.amazon.com/dp/B07XPBPLSR

Other books by Linda West
(Featuring Kissing Bridge and the Landers)

The Magical Christmas Do- Over
Christmas Kisses and Cookies
Holiday Wishes and Valentine Kisses
Olympic Wishes and Kisses
Firework Kisses and Summertime Wishes
Paris Kisses and Christmas Wishes
Christmas Belles and Mistletoe
Christmas at the Cozy Café
My Billionaire Fake Fiance
Mystery
Death by Crockpot
Death by Rolling Pin

Thank you so much for reading my books! I hope you and your family have a wonderful and very merry Christmas!
Truly,
Linda West

Would you like to join our friends and family group to be notified for future releases and sales? We love our readers and we never spam. As a FREE GIFT we'll send you Linda's best selling Christmas novel featuring the Landers and their magical recipes.

Christmas Kisses and Cookies

FOR FREE
Just write us at Morningmayan@gmail.com
And join our wonderful little online family!

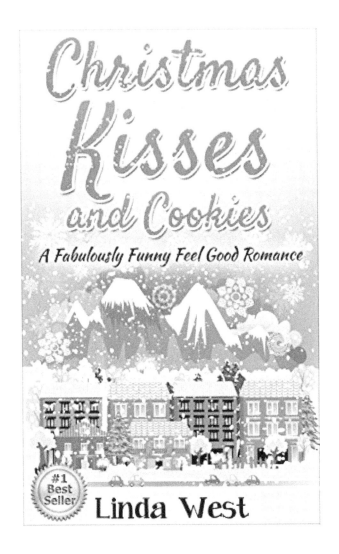

The complete set of Love on Kissing Bridge Mountain series is available NOW on Amazon.

Do you like cozy mysteries? See what's on the menu at the Enchanted Café when a crockpot goes missing at the big chili cook-off and a body is found. Featuring the Landers and their magical recipe book!

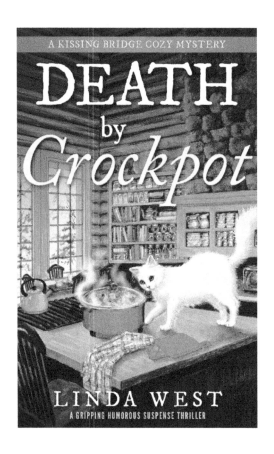

#1 Best Seller in humor and cozy culinary mysteries

The follow up Enchanted Café Mystery. Another humorous cozy murder featuring the wonderful Landers ladies and magical friends.

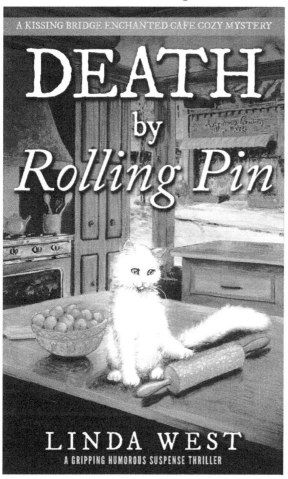

Thank you so much for reading my books!
Also special thanks to Jocelyn Gibson for her
wonderful art and Shea Megale for her editing.

Wishing you a wonderful holiday season!!!

Made in the USA
Coppell, TX
27 October 2020

40371296R00226